ENGLAND'S TOUGHEST VILLAIN

ENGLAND'S TOUGHEST VILLAIN

Joe Cannon

THE LEMON BOOK CO. LTD.

First published 1989 by
The Lemon Book Co. Ltd.
10 St. Ann's Villas, London W11 4RX

British Library Cataloguing in Publication Data
Cannon, Joe
England's toughest villain.
I. Title
823'.914 [F]

ISBN 1-871595-01-0

Typeset by Goodfellow & Egan Ltd., Cambridge
Printed and bound in Great Britain by Bookcraft Ltd.,

To my daughter Kim and to my grandchildren;
may they grow up in a better world.

Foreword

Although founded on fact, the characters and episodes in this book bear no relation to real persons, either living or dead, and are entirely the product of the Author's imagination. Only when reference is made to actual happenings are real names and places mentioned.

The Author
London 1989

Contents

1. *The Return of Joey Bello*

The flame-red Alfa Romeo Spyder sped down the motorway leading to Gatwick airport. The hood was down and the driver's long blonde hair cascaded in the wind. Hands resting lightly on the wheel, the young woman drove with an expert touch that smacked of the race-track.

She was extraordinarily beautiful, oval-faced with an aristocratic nose and full lips. She wore the minimum of make-up, her skin was lightly tanned. The eyes scanning the road ahead were dark blue and intense.

The telephone call from Spain had come through the previous evening and she was now on her way to a meeting which she was certain would change her life. The daughter of an eminent QC, her mother a successful writer of romantic novels, she had been brought up in the lap of luxury. A first-class education had culminated in an honours degree; she had been able to take her pick from a variety of jobs and she had chosen advertising as a career in which she hoped to find fulfilment and the excitement she craved. Now a highly-paid accounts executive with an international company, a Mayfair flat and an unlimited expense allowance, she was nevertheless dissatisfied.

The man who had phoned from Spain asking her to meet him at Gatwick was a pleasantly-remembered memory. They had met in a West End night club to which she had been taken in the wake of a charity ball. Her escort, a chinless wonder who was heir to a dukedom and a considerable fortune, had been selected by her parents as a possible suitor. He bored her to tears.

The fight started soon after the pair had been seated at a table on the edge of the small dance floor. The man who plucked her from the mêlée, while the chinless wonder stood by helplessly, was something new in her life. She could well have taken care of herself, for she was a black belt karate and a third Dan Judokai, but that was irrelevant. She was impressed by the decisive way her rescuer had performed, his utter fearlessness in the face of danger and the speed with which he whisked her away from the battleground.

'May I drive you home,' he had said. He had an attractive voice with a slight Cockney accent.

'Yes, please,' she said.

The chinless wonder mustered up a little courage.

'What about me?' he moaned.

'What about you, Charlie?' she said. 'You can fuck off.'

The man drove her home. On the front steps of the block of flats in Park Lane they exchanged names and telephone numbers. He shook her hand, said 'Good night, Duchess,' and drove off into the night. Somehow she felt that he had left behind a gap in her life.

The sign said AIRPORT, and she swung the Spyder into the slip road. On the open space in front of the main entrance, where No Parking signs proliferated, she slid the car expertly into a vacant slot, switched off the engine and slid out of the driving seat with a tantalising display of very shapely leg. As she moved towards the entrance to the concourse, walking with the lithe grace of a ballet dancer, a uniformed attendant moved to intercept her. She flashed him a brilliant smile.

'Shan't be long,' she said. 'Keep an eye on my car, won't you.'

The attendant, his air of authority crumbling, was incapable of speech. Dumbly he nodded and watched her progress as she passed out of sight.

The man sitting in the rear section of the Boeing 737 as it entered air space above Gatwick could have been anybody from a diplomatic messenger to an international businessman. His lightweight suit in a dark blue material was expensively tailored, the silk shirt and Gucci tie impeccable.

He glanced at the gold Rolex on his left wrist. The time was two-thirty.

The passport in his inside pocket described him as Frank Masterton, manufacturer's agent, and the photograph showed a bearded face which, even in monochrome, appeared deeply tanned. The illuminated sign above his seat read 'NO SMOKING. FASTEN SEAT BELTS'. The aircraft slowly circled and came in to land.

As the landing wheels made contact with the runway and the engines went into reverse thrust, he thought about the impending meeting on which so much depended. Would she be there? She had sounded very positive on the phone but, as he well knew, Fate had a habit of playing strange tricks. He put the doubts out of his head and, picking up the briefcase at his side, prepared to disembark.

Immigration presented no problem. The official glanced at his passport, gave him no more than a cursory glance and waved him through. He had travelled without baggage, and he was able to head straight for the Green channel and reach Customs well ahead of his fellow passengers. Walking briskly, he had almost reached the end of the channel when an official appeared from nowhere. The conversation was brief.

'Good afternoon, sir. No baggage?'

'No.'

'You have nothing to declare?'

'Nothing.'

For a moment the eyes of the two men met, then the look of suspicion faded.

'Very well. Thank you, sir.'

It was a doddle. The man passed through the sliding doors leading to the exit and saw her immediately, the beautiful face framed by the mass of blonde hair, the trim figure in the tailored coat and skirt, the broad smile displaying perfect teeth.

As he reached the barrier she came to him and they briefly touched hands.

'Welcome home, Joey Bello,' said Francesca Smithson-Wright.

'Hallo, Duchess,' said Joey Bello.

'The beard doesn't suit you,' she said.

'It'll be gone by tomorrow.'

Comfortably ensconced in the airport bar, Joey ordered a bottle of Dom Perignon and the two settled down to talk. She came to the point quickly.

'What's on your mind, Joey?'

'Quite a lot, Duchess,' he said. 'I've been thinking about you, wondering about you . . .'

'So. Let's not mess around. You've got some sort of proposition. Out with it.'

Joey pondered a moment, his dark eyes fixed on her face.

'First off, can I ask you a few questions?'

'Go ahead.'

'How old are you and what do you do for a living?'

'I'm twenty-five. I'm an accounts executive with the Delbert brothers.'

'Do you like your job?'

She exploded. 'Look, Joey, cut out the shit. You're up to something. Whatever it is, it's got to be better than pissing around in the advertising racket. Put your cards on the table.'

'Take it easy, Duchess,' said Joey. 'Take it easy. Tell me, what do you know about me?'

She pondered the question for a moment.

'I'll tell you. You did a disappearing act. I wondered why, so I asked around. Don't worry, it was very discreet. You're a villain who's got on the wrong side of some very important people. They think they've got rid of you. When you pop up again, they'll try to do something about it. Right?'

'Right.'

'You've been out in Spain for a few months. My guess is you've made a lot of money. Now you're back. What are you after? Revenge?'

'Amongst other things – yes.'

'OK. So where do I fit in?'

Joey sipped his champagne and looked at her steadily. In that moment they knew more about each other than they would have done over twenty-four hours of question and answer.

'OK, I'll come to the point,' said Joey. 'I need you. You're an educated lady. You move in the best circles. Your father is Sir Alec Smithson-Wright QC. Your mother is Lady Fiona Smithson-Wright, a successful authoress . . .'

'My father is a pompous prick and my mother writes shit which somehow sells. Now carry on.'

'I stand corrected,' said Joey, smiling. 'Anyway, here's my proposition. I'm going to set up as a private eye and I'd like you to come in with me, equal partners. What do you say?'

'When do we start?'

'What's wrong with right now?' said Joey.

'Fine. Throw away your moody passport, shave off that lousy beard and let's go.'

'Are you sure you want to do this? It'll be tough.'

'Sure I'm sure,' said Francesca. 'Come on, let's go.'

'How about finishing off the shampoo?' said Joey.

She looked at the half-empty bottle of Dom Perignon.

'Leave it for the waiter,' said the Duchess, regally. 'He probably won't appreciate it, but he'll drink it just the same.'

Together they emerged into the sunshine of the June afternoon. The uniformed attendant, a smile on his face, was lounging in the vicinity of the Spyder. The smile changed to a scowl when he saw Joey, but his expression brightened as he took the fiver which was thrust into his not unwilling hand. Francesca eased herself into the driving seat, Joey tucked himself in beside her, the engine burst into life and within minutes they were on the motorway en route for London.

The Bolinbroke Hotel is a small but select establishment within a few minutes' walk of Kensington High Street. The proprietor, a wheeler and dealer in the property market, who had made a fortune by the time he reached his fiftieth birthday, was an old friend whose discretion could be relied upon. Francesca dropped Joey at the door.

'Give you a bell about seven, OK?' said Joey.

'Fine. See you,' she said.

The Spyder roared off. Joey went up the steps to the entrance, pushed open the door and walked in.

The lounge was deep-carpeted and tastefully furnished. Directly opposite the entrance was the reception desk, behind which sat an elderly woman with carefully groomed hair and a kindly expression. She gave Joey a welcoming smile.

'Good afternoon, sir,' she said. 'Can I help you?'

'Mister O'Malley,' said Joey.

'Who shall I say wants him?'

'Tell him it's Joey Bello.'

'Just a moment, sir. I'll see if he's available.'

The receptionist disappeared through a door marked PRIVATE. Almost immediately the door re-opened and a tall, distinguished-looking man with a mane of white hair emerged. He bounced out of the reception area and enfolded Joey in a bear hug.

'Joey, me old china,' he said. 'How bloody nice to see you.'

'Likewise,' said Joey. 'How've you been, Kevin?'

'Never better, my son, never better. Don't let's stand here. Come into the inner sanctum.'

O'Malley leading the way, the two men passed through the door leading to the private office. It was a man's room in which everything had been sacrificed to comfort: deep leather armchairs, a capacious settee, thick pile carpets and, the only concession to business, an elegant desk by the single large window.

O'Malley, his six foot height topping Joey's by a couple of inches, propelled his guest to the settee.

'Sit you down there, me boy, and I'll get you a touch of the malt that'll delight the soul of you,' he said. He went to an adjacent table bearing an array of bottles, selected one without a label and poured two liberal measures. Handing one of the glasses to Joey, he draped himself in one of the armchairs. He raised his glass and Joey followed suit.

'Now then,' said O'Malley, 'tell me what's been happening to you. A little bird told me you were in sunny Spain making a fortune.'

'Didn't do badly,' said Joey. 'Ran into Micky and Ron out there. They send their regards.'

'Ah, yes. Very bright boys those two. Making plenty are they?'

'Not doing too badly.'

'Good. Always pleased to hear of somebody doing well. So, Joey, what can I do for you?'

'I need to be somewhere quiet for about a couple of weeks,' said Joey. 'How are you fixed?'

'Couldn't have come at a better time, my son. My best suite's empty. It's yours for as long as you want it.'

'Lead me to it,' said Joey.

The best suite was a luxurious first floor apartment comprising two bedrooms, a sitting-room and a magnificent bathroom. It looked out over the central garden of a square with shady trees and green, well-tended lawns.

'Now, me boy,' said Kevin. 'Just make yourself at home. I'll let the staff know that you're me special guest. Anything you need, just ring for it. Come down and join me for a little drink when you're ready.'

'Thanks, Kevin,' said Joey. 'You're a diamond.'

After a hot bath and a somewhat painful ten minutes getting rid of his whiskers, Joey spent the best part of an hour on the phone, at the end of which time he had arranged for a complete wardrobe to be supplied from London's foremost department store. A call to a friend who managed an estate agency in the West End left him with the assurance that, by the morrow, he would have a comprehensive list of houses for sale within a radius of a mile of Oxford Circus. Then, placing a call to be awakened at six-thirty, he collapsed onto the bed in the larger bedroom and fell asleep.

The first tinkle of the bell of the internal telephone and he was awake, hand outstretched to lift the receiver from its cradle. He had always been able to emerge from a cat-nap into instant wakefulness, all senses alert.

He took a quick shower, ran the razor over his face again and fingered the scar that furrowed his cheek. Already it showed signs of fading and would, he knew from experience, soon be almost imperceptible.

The department store had lived up to its reputation, the boxes bearing the famous name were stacked neatly in the sitting-room, and he spent a pleasant few minutes opening them and spreading the contents on the furniture. He selected a dark suit, a white silk shirt and a sober tie, dressed rapidly and inspected the final result in the full-length mirror in the bedroom. Everything fitted to perfection. At seven o'clock precisely he called the Mayfair number.

Her voice came to him, cool and unflurried, a quiet 'hello'.

'Joey,' he said.

'I know,' she replied.

'Dinner tonight?'

'Fine.'

'Pick you up at eight. OK?'

'I'll be waiting.'

The line went dead. Joey left the suite, carefully locking the door behind him, and went down the stairs to the lounge. The same receptionist was on duty and greeted him with the pleasant smile which seemed to be a fixture on her face.

'Good evening, sir,' she said.

'Evening,' said Joey. 'Thanks for taking in those parcels for me. How much do I owe you?'

'Mister O'Malley attended to that, sir. He told me to say he was in the bar, and would you join him.'

'I'll do that. Now, I shall want a car with driver for the evening. Can you arrange it?'

'Certainly, sir. What time?'

'Quarter to eight?'

'Yes sir. It will be waiting for you.'

Joey strolled into the bar, a pleasant room with discreet lighting and comfortable furnishings. The large French windows gave on to a spacious patio where some of the guests were taking their aperitifs. Kevin O'Malley, perched on a stool at the far end of the bar, beckoned to Joey to join him.

'What'll you have?' he said.

'A touch of your special malt would go down very well.'

O'Malley raised a finger to the white-coated barman, using the same finger to indicate his own glass.

'The same, sir?' said the barman and, at O'Malley's nod, brought up an unlabelled bottle from a recess below the bar counter and poured a generous measure into a crystal goblet. The two men raised their glasses to each other.

'Settling in all right?' O'Malley asked.

'Very comfortable. By the way, you took some gear in for me. How much do I owe you?'

His host made an expansive gesture. 'Not to worry, me boy. We'll settle up at the end of your stay with us.'

'As you like,' said Joey. O'Malley was being very accommodating, he thought. There couldn't have been much change out of three grand for that little lot from the top people's store. Pushing back his cuff, he glanced at the Rolex.

'Going out?' said O'Malley.

'Yeah. Got a meet on. Probably be late back.'

'No trouble. Just ring the bell. We've got a night security man. He's very good.'

Joey finished his drink and smacked his lips appreciatively.

'One for the road?'

'Thanks. Another time. A little of that stuff goes a long way.'

'Hasta luego, senor,' said O'Malley.

Joey looked him in the eye. He grinned wolfishly.

'Why don't you speak English, you Spanish pillock,' he said.

O'Malley was still roaring with laughter as Joey left the bar.

The driver was waiting at the reception desk, a small man in a smart grey uniform, the matching cap tucked beneath his arm. Joey recognised him immediately – Adgie Wheels, the finest getaway driver in the business. There was no flicker of recognition in the little man's eyes.

'Your car, sir,' he said.

He preceded Joey onto the pavement and opened the rear door of the car, a shining Daimler limousine. Joey sank back into the cushioned interior.

'Where to, sir?' said the little man.

'Fountain Towers, Park Lane,' said Joey.

The car slid away from the kerb and headed in the direction of Knightsbridge. Through the partly-open partition window Joey spoke to the man behind the wheel.

'How are you, Adgie?'

'Fine and dandy, Joey. You?'

'Never better. What's the word?'

'I'm on Kevin's firm. On call to the Bolinbroke. Nice steady work. Good money.'

'I'll be using you. Best behaviour tonight, eh?'

'Best behaviour . . . sir.'

The journey was short. The Daimler drew up outside Fountain Towers and Adgie was out of the driving seat in a flash, holding the passenger door open and standing to attention as Joey alighted.

In the vestibule the security man was deferential but firm.

'Who did you wish to see, sir?' he said.

'Miss Smithson-Wright. She's expecting me.'

The man picked up a phone, pressed a button and murmured a few words into the mouthpiece. He turned to Joey.

'Miss Smithson-Wright will be down in a moment, sir,' he said.

Less than a minute later the doors of the elevator opened and Francesca emerged, looking as if she had just stepped out of the pages of a fashion magazine. Her red satin dress contrasted sharply with the gold of her hair and the white linen coat draped casually over her shoulders. Joey piloted her to the waiting car.

Adgie, playing his part to perfection, was on hand to usher them into their seats.

'Where to, sir?' he said.

'Ace of Diamonds, Islington Green. You know it?'

'Yes, sir.'

The passenger door closed with an almost inaudible click. Adgie took his place behind the wheel and the Daimler eased its way into the traffic stream.

Relaxed in the deep upholstery, a smile curving her lips, Francesca surveyed her companion.

'The beard's gone. Quite an improvement,' she said.

'It was only what you might call temporary cover,' said Joey, returning the smile.

'You're a bit pale round the jowls. May I suggest a touch of the sun lamp?'

'That'll be attended to in due course.'

'Excellent. Now, where are you taking me?'

'A very nice place where you'll meet a most interesting man.'

'I love meeting interesting people,' she said.

The Daimler was negotiating the roundabout at Piccadilly Circus. Joey smiled as he remembered the last time he had been a passenger in a car driven by Adgie. The attempted prison break had gone wrong and it was a question of getting out of a tight spot. Driving a powerful Jaguar, Adgie had put the car through a series of tests which the makers had never envisaged.

'Why do you smile?' asked Francesca.

'Memories. Just memories,' said Joey. 'Tell you about them later.'

The Daimler purred along Shaftesbury Avenue, into Theobald's Road, through Clerkenwell and on to the Angel at Islington, finally coming to a halt in front of a heavily-curtained establishment whose exterior gave no hint of what went on beyond the massive oak door leading to the inside. The watchful eye of a closed-circuit telecamera mounted above the door indicated that the premises were very private indeed.

Adgie was quickly out of his seat. He opened the door, cap off and tucked beneath his arm. With his free hand he helped Francesca to alight. Joey followed her, pausing to press a tenner into the little man's receptive grasp.

'Come back about midnight. Park up and wait for us,' said Joey.

'Very good, sir,' said Adgie.

The Ace of Diamonds was among the ten best restaurants in London, though its name did not appear in the Good Food Guide, nor was it publicised in the glossy magazines. Its reputation was built on the personality of the owner, a tall, slim and incredibly good-looking West Indian who was known to his exclusive clientele simply as Ace.

Many famous names and faces had passed through the oaken door. Here the cream of London's villains rubbed shoulders with stars of stage, screen and television. The food was superb, the service smooth and efficient and the menu and wine list carried no prices. Ace charged his customers what he thought they could afford and, in the rare case of complaint, the bill was torn up and the complainer informed that he was no longer persona grata.

The arrival of the Daimler had been observed, the occupant identified and the heavy oak door swung open as they reached it. They came into the restaurant proper through a secondary door, and the proprietor was there in person to welcome them.

'Joey,' said Ace Johnson. There was no mistaking the joy in the soft West Indian voice nor the warmth with which he slapped palms, Caribbean fashion.

'Hiya, Ace,' said Joey. He turned to his companion.

'Duchess, I'd like to introduce you to Ace Johnson, a good friend. Ace, meet the Duchess.'

Ace took Francesca's hand, brushing it with his lips.

'Welcome to my humble joint, beautiful lady,' he said. 'May this be the first of many visits.'

'How could I stay away?' she said.

Ace beamed with delight. 'Come along, my friends,' he said. 'Take the weight off your feet.'

He led them to a secluded table in a remote corner of the room. Francesca's coat was spirited away by an attentive waiter, who must have received a secret signal from his employer, for he re-appeared almost at once carrying an ice-bucket containing a bottle of Dom Perignon which he stood in a cradle next to the table. Ace did the honours. With an ease born of long practice he opened the bottle, filled three glasses and drew up a chair.

'I'll join you for a few minutes,' he said. 'It's not every day that one welcomes home an old friend.'

This opening gambit set the standard for the meal that was to follow. Ace hovered unobtrusively in the background as his guests did full justice to the food. The wines were superb and the service faultless. When the time came for coffee to be served, Ace produced a bottle of very old Armagnac.

While they were eating conversation had been sparse and mostly confined to comments on the excellence of the food and drink. Now, well wined and dined, over their glasses of Armagnac, they talked.

'Any more views on my proposition, Duchess?' said Joey.

'I've already said I'm in. You could answer one question though.'

'What is it?'

'I'd like to know if you're just using me to get what you want. Not that it makes any difference. I'm in, whatever you say.'

Joey pondered briefly. It was a question he had been expecting and he knew he must answer it honestly.

'Everybody uses everybody, Duchess,' he said. 'Maybe, subconsciously, I'm trying to use you. I won't kid you. Anyway, you're far too intelligent to be easily fooled. Let's put it this way. We're partners, and we're responsible to each other. Can we go from there?'

'That suits me, Joey,' she said. 'I'm a big girl, and I'll take the responsibility for my decisions. That way I've nobody else to blame but myself. So we go from here.'

'Right. This is the plan. We've got to have a base, so I'm going house-hunting tomorrow. Like to come along?'

'Try and keep me away.'

'Wouldn't think of it. What time shall I pick you up in the morning?'

'Nine o'clock?'

'Fine.'

'By the way,' she said, 'does Ace have any place in your strategy?'

'At a later stage, yes. I've known him since we were kids in Notting Dale. I'd trust him with my life.'

'So let me get to know him a little.'

Every restaurateur worth his salt possesses a sixth sense which tells him that his presence may be needed. That sense was highly developed in Ace Johnson. Hardly were the words out of Francesca's mouth than Ace appeared, smiling all over his face.

'How was the meal?' he said.

'Don't talk bloody rubbish,' said Joey. 'You know it was out of this world. Anyway, we were just talking about you. Sit down and have some of this jungle juice.'

'Hark to the peasant,' said Ace. 'He refers to a priceless Armagnac as jungle juice.'

Ace drew up a chair and helped himself to the Armagnac. He sipped it with enjoyment.

'You and Joey have known each other for a long time,' said Francesca.

Ace looked at Joey. There was a question in his eyes.

'It's OK. Me and the Duchess are partners,' said Joey. 'No secrets from each other.'

They fell into an easy, three-sided conversation and, as the level in the bottle of Armagnac lowered, so the friendly atmosphere became more friendly. Joey and Ace talked about the old days in Notting Dale, Francesca listened and occasionally interjected a few words. Finally Joey looked at his watch.

'After midnight, Duchess. We've a heavy day tomorrow. Shall we make a move?'

'You're the boss, Joey,' she said.

Ace escorted them to the door. The shining Daimler was parked outside with Adgie in attendance. They said their goodnights to Ace and the Daimler moved smoothly into the light traffic of the early morning.

At the entrance to Fountain Towers Joey briefly took Francesca's hand.

'See you in the morning. Nine o'clock,' he said.

'Fine. Thanks for a lovely evening, Joey.'

At the Bolinbroke Joey made arrangements with Adgie to be picked up at eight-thirty the following day. He went straight up to the suite, undressed rapidly, climbed into bed and was asleep within seconds.

Breakfast at the Bolinbroke left Joey in no doubt as to his standing there. He ploughed his way through an enormous dish of perfectly-cooked bacon and eggs, munched hot toast with Oxford marmalade and drank a couple of cups of delicious coffee. Then, fortified for the day, he left the dining room.

Adgie was waiting by the reception desk, the model chauffeur, hair slicked back, shoes highly polished and his uniform cap tucked under his arm. He led the way to the Daimler parked at the kerb and ushered Joey inside.

'Where to, sir?' he said as he took his place behind the wheel.

'Fountain Towers,' said Joey. 'And don't bother about the "sir" business when there's nobody about.'

'Right, Joey,' said Adgie and set the car in motion.

At the Towers Joey went through the usual rigmarole with security.

'Miss Smithson-Wright asks if you would care to go up to the flat?' said the security man.

'Certainly,' said Joey.

The man murmured into the phone.

'The first lift over there, sir,' he said. 'Flat two on the third floor. It's right opposite the lift as you get out.'

'Thanks,' said Joey.

The door of the flat opened almost as soon as he had pressed the bell push.

'Come in,' said Francesca. 'I thought you might like to see my pad.'

Joey walked into the spacious hallway as Francesca closed the door.

'Go through,' she said. 'The door right in front of you.'

The sitting-room on the other side of the door could only be described as palatial. Huge French windows occupied the whole of one side of the room where a balcony gave on to a view of Hyde Park. The deep white carpet was wall-to-wall and four capacious easy-chairs with two matching settees were ranged round a large, glass-topped occasional table. The plain white walls were embellished with a half-dozen paintings which, even to Joey's inexpert eye, were original works of art chosen with great care to blend in with their surroundings. In a corner was a well-stocked bar.

Francesca had followed him into the room.

'Like it?' she said.

'Very nice. Very nice indeed,' said Joey.

She pointed in turn to the three doors leading off the sitting room.

'Bedroom and en-suite bathroom in there,' she said. 'Kitchen there. Second bath and usual offices there. Would you like a conducted tour?'

'I'll take your word for it,' said Joey. 'Right now I'd like to get down to business.'

Francesca smiled. 'You'll have a coffee?'

Without waiting for an answer she went to the occasional table where a coffee pot and two cups were arranged on a tray.

'Pick yourself a chair,' she said as she poured the coffee.

Joey sat in one of the easy-chairs and took out the sheaf of papers which he had received that morning. Francesca pulled up another chair and sat beside him. He spread the agent's particulars on the table.

'I've only glanced through these, Duchess,' he said. 'Let's go over them together.'

The next ten minutes were spent immersed in estate agents' hyperbole, then Francesca sat back in her chair.

'What do you think?' asked Joey.

'Out of that lot, two possibilities,' replied Francesca. 'The place in Fitzroy Square and the house in Park Lane. So far as I'm concerned, Park Lane is favourite.'

'Exactly what I thought,' said Joey. 'Let's have a butcher's.'

The house at the north end of Park Lane was a substantial Georgian edifice fronted by a small patio. It consisted of a large basement and two upper floors. At the rear, with access from the basement, was a paved yard surrounded by high walls. The premises were in an excellent state of repair, the paintwork good and all the windows were double-glazed. Standing in the ground floor front room, the traffic noises from Park Lane only a muted hum, Joey outlined his plans.

'The basement will be a fully equipped gym where we can do work-outs and keep ourselves in trim,' he said. 'This ground floor will be the offices of the agency. Upstairs will be my private quarters. What do you think, Duchess?'

'Agreed,' Francesca replied.

'Good. I'll do the necessary and get the builders in.'

'It's going to cost you a packet,' said Francesca.

'I've got a packet,' replied Joey.

2. *The House in Park Lane*

The quiet and calm of a gentlemen's club in St. James's is an ideal place for contemplation. The man who sat in a secluded corner of the lounge was certainly in a thoughtful mood. He sipped from a cup of black coffee, occasionally glancing at his watch and looking towards the door.

When his expected visitor finally arrived he could not conceal his impatience.

'What the hell's been keeping you, Gill,' he snapped. 'We had an appointment for eleven o'clock.'

The newcomer looked at his watch.

'My dear Finch,' he said, 'it is now precisely three minutes past eleven. Pull yourself together, man. And may I remind you that you're not speaking to one of your subordinates at the Yard. Keep your ill-mannered remarks for them. They can't answer back.'

Doctor Matthew Gill lowered himself into a comfortable leather armchair as a steward approached the table.

'I would like black coffee,' he said. 'The Mocha. And Hennessy, please.'

'The XO, sir?'

'Of course. What about you, Finch?'

'I'm all right as I am,' was the ungracious reply.

The steward padded away and Gill leaned back in his chair, crossing one impeccably-tailored leg over the other.

'Now, Finch,' he said. 'What's the panic? From the tone of your voice when you phoned I thought the world was coming to an end.'

'Cut out the sarcasm, Gill. It's bad news.'

Gill laughed. 'When the messenger comes bearing bad news, kill the messenger,' he said.

The other man was almost beside himself with fury.

'For Christ's sake, Gill,' he said. 'Can't you be serious? We're in trouble.'

'So what's the trouble?'

'Bello's back in London.'

'Bello?'

'The fellow who nicked the tapes from your mews place.'

The expression on Doctor Matthew Gill's handsome face underwent a sudden change.

'You told me he had been killed in an accident. So what happened?'

'It's obvious. He got away.'

'Where to?'

Their conversation was interrupted as the steward served Gill's coffee and brandy. He went off and Finch continued.

'So far as we know, somewhere near Marbella in Spain. He had a number of friends out there.'

'And you, Commander Finch, with the resources of what has been described as the finest police force in the world, let this miserable little sneak-thief slip through your fingers?'

The Commander's face darkened with fury.

'Listen to me, Gill. Bello is no miserable sneak-thief. He's a hard man, tough and resourceful. Officially there's no way I can touch him. He's done his crime and served his time.'

Gill picked up his brandy glass and swallowed the contents in one gulp. He drained his coffee cup and rose to his feet.

'And now you listen to me, Commander Finch,' he said. 'Get rid of this man Bello. Get rid of him. If anything, anything at all, happens to me, I'll drag the lot of you down with me, you, and your friends, Cabinet Ministers, members of the House of Lords, respected public figures, the whole damned boiling lot of you. Think well on it.'

He turned to go. Over his shoulder he said, 'Don't bother about the bill, my dear fellow. I'll settle it.'

Finch watched the Doctor's back as Gill went out of the

room. By the living God, he thought, if I get out of this mess I'll make the insufferable bastard pay dearly for his insults.

A week later the house in Park Lane was almost ready for occupation. Teams of builders, decorators and security experts had worked round the clock to turn the premises into a miniature fortress. Joey and Francesca stood in the centre of the basement floor which had been extended by knocking down the party walls into one large room.

'This is where we'll have the punch-ball and the punch-bag,' said Joey, pointing to a corner. 'Then in the middle we'll have the mat. Parallel bars against the wall over there.'

'No shooting range?' enquired Francesca.

'No guns,' said Joey. 'Shooters are nasty, messy things. They make a lot of noise and don't do any real damage unless one bullet hits a vital spot. All this about drawing and firing and the bloke drops dead is a lot of bullshit.'

'Pity,' said Francesca. 'That is one area of my life where I would have liked a bit of tuition.'

'Leave it out, Duchess,' said Joey. 'I'll teach you a few tricks that don't figure in the manuals on karate and judo.'

'I'm looking forward to that,' said his partner.

They mounted the stairs to the ground floor where Joey gave Francesca a run-down on the various security devices which had been installed.

'From the outside it's a normal front door,' he said. 'No letter box. All mail accepted at this door. Under the paint, three-quarter inch sheet steel.'

He reached up and touched a switch. A picture came up on the adjoining television screen showing a section of the road immediately outside the front door.

'Closed circuit television camera,' he said. 'Limited sweep but enough to show who's at the door and anybody who's with them. Screens in all rooms, including the basement. What do you think?'

'Looks as though you've taken care of everything so far,' said Francesca.

'Good. Now come this way, please.' He opened the door from the hallway leading into the front room.

'This is the main office and reception,' he said. 'Usual office furnishings. Switchboard with connections to all rooms.'

He opened the door to the rear part of the ground floor and Francesca followed him as he went through.

'This room is where the staff will operate. Typing, filing and so on. Telex, copying, it'll all be done here.'

Said Francesca with a smile, 'And what about the loo?'

Joey gestured toward the far end of the room.

'Two toilets. One men, one women. Shower, bidet, hand basin.'

'Fine. What's that room over there?'

'I'll show you,' said Joey.

He entered the room, Francesca close on his heels.

'This is the control room, what you might call the nerve centre of the operation,' he said. 'Look out of the window.'

Francesca went over to the heavily-barred window with its armoured glass and looked out on to the patio. As she did so, Joey touched a switch. The whole of the outside area was brilliantly illuminated.

'Concealed floodlights,' said Joey. 'A mouse couldn't hide out there.'

Francesca laughed. 'Don't tell me you're afraid of mice,' she said.

'Depends how many there are,' said Joey. He gestured toward one wall of the room which was a mass of instruments, including four television screens.

'From here you can see everything that goes on in the house and the street outside,' he said. 'Nice little set-up, eh?'

Francesca nodded. 'What's upstairs?' she said.

'My private domain,' said Joey. 'Come on and I'll show you.'

Joey leading the way, they climbed the stairs to the first floor where they emerged on to a small landing. To their left was a door, its plain painted surface innocent of any trace of locks or other protective devices. Joey put his hand in his pocket and the door swung open.

'After you, Duchess,' he said.

They came into a fairly spacious hallway. The door swung closed behind them.

'What's this?' enquired Francesca. 'Black magic?'

Joey took his hand from his pocket and opened it to disclose a small black box, slightly less bulky than a cigarette packet.

'Electronics. The wonder of the age. This little gadget opens all the doors in the place,' he said. 'Over-rides the security and cuts out the alarms.'

He put his hand in his pocket and took out a replica of the box.

'This is yours, Duchess,' he said. 'There's only two of them, so take care of it.'

'I'll guard it with my life,' she said.

Two doors led off the hallway, one to the right and one to the left. Joey pushed the left-hand door and stood aside as Francesca entered the room overlooking the park. It was a man's room, simply furnished, well-carpeted with a few prints on the plain white walls.

'Like it?' asked Joey.

'Neat but not gaudy,' replied Francesca. 'What's in the other room?'

'Sleeping quarters. Come and have a look.'

He led the way across the hall into the room which looked out on the rear patio. Here again the surroundings were austere and practical, a comfortable bed, a bedside table on which stood two telephones, a dressing table, two easy chairs and a wardrobe which occupied the whole of one wall. Joey jerked a thumb in the direction of one corner.

'Bathroom in there,' he said.

'No kitchen?' she said.

'Too much bother,' replied Joey. 'We've got round the clock security, eight-hour shifts. The bloke on duty can deal with the odd tea or coffee. Otherwise I'll eat out.'

Francesca smiled mischievously.
'What about crumpet?'
Joey laughed. 'No crumpet up here,' he said. 'Rest and relaxation only. Any more questions?'
'Just one. Does the little magic gadget open the front door?'
'No. That can only be opened from the inside.'
'Supposing something happens to the security man? A heart attack – something like that?'
Joey frowned. 'I never thought of that,' he said. 'No sweat. I'll get our gadgets modified so that they'll work on the front door as well.'
'Good. Where do we go from here?'
Joey looked at his watch.
'I've got to meet with the architect and the builders right now,' he said. 'All the gear is being delivered tomorrow. The day after we're in business.'
The architect and his builders were most co-operative.
'Everything will be in order and working by nine o'clock in the morning the day after tomorrow,' said the architect. 'The electricians will be on hand for a test run. After that it's all yours.'
'Fine,' said Joey. 'See you later, then.'
Outside the front door Francesca paused.
'No nameplate?' she said.
'No nameplate,' replied Joey. 'No need to advertise. I've put the word around. We won't have to look for clients. Now, where would you like to lunch?'
'There's a nice little place in Chelsea.'
'OK. Let's go.'

'Le Rambouillet' is a small but select restaurant off the King's Road. Adgie deposited his passengers outside the front door.
'Couple of hours,' said Joey.
'Very good, sir,' said Adgie.
Joey pushed open the door to allow Francesca to lead the way. As she entered the head waiter, impeccable in black jacket and striped trousers, came forward to greet her.

'Mam'selle Francesca. Nice to see you.'

He gave a slight bow in Joey's direction.

'Good morning, sir. Welcome to Le Rambouillet.'

He turned his attention to Francesca.

'Where would you like to sit, mam'selle?'

The restaurant was not unduly crowded. Francesca indicated a table for two in a quiet corner by the curtained window, and the head waiter ushered them to their seats.

'Don't bother with the menu, Raoul,' she said. 'What's good today?'

Raoul smiled. 'As usual, mam'selle, everything. The Dover sole is excellent. I think you will enjoy it.'

Francesca glanced at Joey, who gave an approving nod. He was content to leave matters in his companion's hands.

'The sole for both of us. Green salad. Some fresh vegetables.'

Raoul scribbled on his order pad and tore off the sheet which he handed to the white-coated waiter at his elbow.

'And to drink, mam'selle?'

Francesca looked over to Joey. 'There's a very good Montrachet,' she said. 'How about it?'

'Fine by me,' said Joey. 'How about a drink while we're waiting?'

'A very dry Martini,' she said.

Joey looked up at Raoul. 'For me, a dry Cinzano. Soda and ice.'

'Certainly, sir. At once,' said Raoul.

The arrival of the pair had not gone unnoticed. At a table in the centre of the room a group of four young men were celebrating. Their coats were draped over the backs of their respective chairs, champagne coolers littered the table and, despite the early hour, they were all slightly drunk. One of them detached himself from his companions and strolled towards Francesca's table, where he came to a halt, swaying slightly.

'Hello, lovely lady,' he said. 'Wouldn't you like more entertaining company? Come and join us.'

Marion flashed him a brilliant smile as she shook his hand. Adgie was captivated immediately and managed to get out three words.

'How are you?' he said.

'All right, Marion,' said Joey. 'Would you like to show us how your department works?'

'Certainly, Mr Bello,' she said, and led the way to a compact switchboard in one corner of the room.

'Ten lines,' she said. 'All incoming and outgoing calls are monitored and recorded and transcribed by word processor. Printed records of conversations transferred to microfilm and stored in the computer memory for instant recall by date and time.'

'Very comprehensive,' said Francesca. Adgie, who had not understood a single word, chimed in with 'Bloody marvellous'.

Marion went on. 'This section is completely automatic. In the event of a power failure the system switches to battery power via a fail-safe device. The changeover is instantaneous.'

'That the lot?' said Joey.

'That's the lot, Mr Bello,' said the girl.

'Good. Now we'll have a look next door. Thanks, Marion.'

'A pleasure, Mr Bello,' she replied.

The trio passed through into the rear office. The three men and two women who were waiting there straightened up as Francesca entered, followed by Joey and Adgie. The women wore overalls in a light blue material, similar to that worn by Marion, a single letter B embroidered on the left breast. The men were garbed in a semi-military uniform of battle-dress and trousers in the same colour as the overalls worn by the women with a similar motif on the left breast.

'Afternoon,' said Joey.

The five replied in chorus. 'Good afternoon, sir.'

'This is the Duchess, my partner. Adgie here is in charge of transport on the firm. OK?'

There was a general nodding of heads. Joey gestured towards the elder of the two women.

'This is Helen,' he said. 'She's in charge of the office. Responsible for keeping the books and general office work. All in order for tomorrow?'

'Yes, Mr Bello,' she said. A handsome woman, dark hair streaked with grey, sharp eyes behind slightly-tinted glasses, she exuded the same brisk air of efficiency as her colleague Marion.

'And this is Jane,' said Joey. 'She's Helen's assistant.'

The girl smiled. She was very pretty, tall and slim, with blonde hair and blue eyes.

'You can tell her what to do in five different languages,' said Joey. 'She speaks 'em all.'

He turned his attention to the three men.

'Duchess, meet Harry, Fred and John,' he said. 'Our security force. On duty round the clock. Eight-hour shifts, seven days a week.'

Francesca gave them an appraising look. There was no doubt in her mind that they were an impressive trio. Harry, the tallest of the three, topped six feet. His colleagues, though shorter, were of the same stamp, hard men who carried themselves with an air that said 'take liberties at your peril'.

She endeared them to her with a simple feminine artifice. She turned on a brilliant smile and raised her right hand in half-salute.

'Hiya, boys,' she said.

They made a rapid tour of the basement. Adgie disappeared, murmuring that he was going to do one or two things to the motor. Joey knew what he meant. The little man would not be satisfied until he had made improvements on the maker's specification and brought the machine to a state of near-perfection.

Francesca tried out the parallel bars and practised a few break-falls on the mat. Joey stood by and watched with a critical eye.

'Very impressive,' he said. 'Bear in mind you might have to deal with something that hits back.' There was a twinkle in his eye.

'I'll cope with that when I come to it,' said Francesca. 'Right now I could do with a refreshing cuppa.'

'No sweat. We'll have it upstairs.'

Over a cup of tea Francesca asked the questions and Joey supplied the answers.

'Give me a breakdown on the staff,' she said.

'Sure. All hand picked. I know them from way back. They have records. Marion was a kiter, passed dud cheques in the West End. Believe it or not, Helen was a screw in Holloway. Ran into trouble, got the sack, did a bit of bird. Jane's her niece. Very well-educated, speaks five languages, French, Spanish, Italian, Greek and Russian. And very good English as well.'

'What about the lads? They look a very useful bunch.'

'All ex-cons. I was with Harry and Fred in Parkhurst. John is Harry's nephew.'

'All with connections in the Dale?'

'That's right. Keeping it in the family as you might say. The villains of Notting Dale have a reputation for sticking together.'

'Well,' said Francesca, 'from where I stand it looks as though you've got everything organised. We go to work tomorrow?'

'Tomorrow, Duchess. By the way, we haven't discussed it yet. How are you fixed for funds?'

'The least of my worries, Joey. If you want me to put something into the firm, just say the word.'

'That's not what I meant. Just want to make sure you don't go short.'

Francesca laughed. 'I don't have to work for wages,' she said. 'Job satisfaction's enough for me. I'm going to enjoy this caper.'

'I hope you do,' said Joey. 'Anyway, I've given Helen her instructions. Anything you want you get. No questions. OK?'

Her answer was feminine and practical and to the point.

'Let's earn some wages first, then we'll talk about housekeeping.'

The intercom set on the occasional table gave out a low-pitched buzz. Joey picked up the handset and listened for a few moments.

'Right,' he said. 'Be down in a couple of minutes.'

He turned to Francesca. 'That was the electrician. He's got our gadgets ready. Come on. Let's try them out on the front door.'

The gadgets worked like a charm.

'Could these be copied?' queried Joey.

The electrician pondered for a few seconds.

'Well,' he said, 'if an electronic expert had a wiring plan of the house and a breakdown of all the security devices inside he might have a ten thousand to one chance.'

'Those sort of odds I like,' said Joey. 'Thanks.'

The electrician went indoors. The watchful Adgie was at the rear door of the Jaguar which seemed to have taken on an added sheen since the morning.

'Motor all right?' said Joey.

'Smashing. I've given the engine a bit of a tickle-up. Running like a piece of silk.'

'Switch on and let's have a listen.'

A gleeful look appeared on the little man's face.

'It's running already,' he said. Joey looked towards the rear of the car where wisps of smoke issued from the twin exhausts.

'You cunning little sod,' he said. 'Get in the car. We'll drop the Duchess at the Towers.'

They walked together up the steps at the entrance to the flats.

'I'm giving a little party on Saturday. Will you be free?' he said.

'Try and keep me away,' she replied. 'Could I invite the parents?'

'They'd be welcome.'

'Thanks. See you tomorrow. Nine o'clock.'

'On the dot.'

Joey returned to the car. He took his place in the front passenger seat. Everything was going well, very well and more than according to plan. Joey felt on top of the world.

'Next stop the Bolinbroke,' he said. As the Jaguar purred away from the kerb and slid into the Park Lane traffic stream, he looked at his watch.

'Five thirty,' he said. 'Kevin will be taking his malt about now.'

Kevin was indeed taking his malt. He greeted Joey with his usual warmth and the barman, needing no instruction, poured out a liberal dose from the unlabelled bottle.

'Now, me boy, how goes it?' asked O'Malley.

'No problems,' said Joey. 'You know my little bash on Saturday. Would you do the catering?'

'If you hadn't mentioned it I would've suggested it. A pleasure, me boy. How many?'

'Say a maximum of fifteen.'

'Good. Dom Perignon shampoo, Chivas Regal whisky, selection of aperitifs . . .'

'Leave it to you, Kevin.'

'You may. I'll send my head chef and a couple of waiters. Albert here will do the bar.'

'Good. That's settled. And don't forget. Bill me for this one.'

'Just as you like. I'm sure we won't fall out.'

'Shouldn't think so,' smiled Joey.

'Now a little matter of business,' said O'Malley. 'Do you remember Morrie Greenbaum?'

'Morrie the jargoon merchant? Sure. What about him?'

'In a big way of business now. Wholesale jewellery. Hatton Garden. I was talking to him this morning.'

'And . . .?'

'He's having a bit of aggravation. I mentioned your name. Said you might be able to help.'

'I will if I can.'

'Here's his private number. Give him a bell.'

Joey took the slip of paper. 'OK, Kevin. I'll be on my way. See you Saturday.'

'If you don't see me, see an oculist,' said O'Malley. He let out a tremendous guffaw.

Joey rang Greenbaum from the coin box in the lobby. The conversation was short. He emerged from the cubicle whistling through his teeth. The tune was 'We're in the money'.

It was nine o'clock. The morning was fine and sunny. The staff of J. Bello Investigations, the architect, the builder and the electricians were assembled to meet him as Joey operated his gadget on the front door and entered the front office. A few moments later Francesca appeared on the scene.

'All ready?' said Joey.

'All ready, Mr Bello,' said the architect.

The final testing of the equipment lasted for a couple of hours. Questions were asked and answered and, at the end of the session, Joey declared himself satisfied.

'You've done a fine job, Mr Brightman,' said Joey.

'Thank you, Mr Bello,' said the architect. 'May I say it's been a pleasure working for you.'

'You may,' said Joey. Both men laughed.

'Now,' said Joey as Brightman and his companions made their exit, 'we're open for business. Let the wagons roll. I've got something on now. Amuse yourself, Duchess. Be back about one.'

Adgie rose to his feet as Joey made for the door.

'Shan't need you, Adgie. You stand by here. I'll take a cab,' said Joey.

Out on Park Lane Joey hailed a taxi.

'Hatton Garden,' he said.

The cabbie, like many of his colleagues, was something of a humourist.

'Going to pick a few flowers, guv'nor?' he said.
'That's right,' said Joey.

Hatton Garden is known throughout the world as the centre of the diamond trade, a big money box where millions of pounds' worth of precious stones are on open display in the windows of the shops which throng both sides of the street. Many more millions are stored in the strong rooms and safes of the dealers, who mainly work from tiny, cramped premises above the shops.

As the cab turned into the Garden from Holborn Circus, Joey rapped on the window.

'Drop me here,' he said.

He paid off the driver and sauntered along the pavement. In a few minutes he reached his destination, a discreetly-curtained establishment with a brass plate on the side of the door which said simply 'Greenbaum'. He pressed the bell push. A disembodied voice came to him through the grille of an intercom.

'Yes,' said the voice.

'Mr Bello. I have an appointment with Mr Greenbaum.'

There was a slight delay, then the door opened to reveal a burly figure in the uniform of a security guard.

'Come this way, sir,' said the guard.

Joey followed the man to the rear of the shop. They came to a tiny lift, large enough to carry one person in comfort.

'If you'd step in, sir,' said the guard, 'you'll be met on the next floor.'

Morrie Greenbaum himself was waiting as the lift shuddered to a stop. Short, fat, bald-headed, very Jewish and extravagant in speech and gesture, he seized Joey's hand and pumped it vigorously.

'Joey, my son. You look marvellous. You're doing well, eh? They treating you right?'

'Mustn't grumble. Earning a crust,' said Joey.

'Come through, come through,' said the little man and led

the way into an office, the main feature of which was a huge safe.

'Sit down, Joey. Make yourself comfortable. Tea? Coffee? Scotch?'

'Nothing just now, Morrie. What's on your mind?'

'What's on my mind? You ask me, I'll tell you. Mr Gladwyn's on my mind.'

'Who's Mr Gladwyn?'

'On the retail side. Shops all over the country. He's been a good customer. Three months' credit, accounts paid on the dot. Now a little bird tells me that he's been setting up moody companies, putting out big orders.'

Joey gave a short laugh. 'The old long firm, eh. Thought it was a bit played out by now. What's he into your ribs for?'

'A hundred grand. Give or take a few quid. Not a lot. So, money I don't like to lose.'

Joey made a shrewd guess that Gladwyn owed fifty or sixty grand. Morrie would put on the frighteners, pay out ten per cent for collection and come out well on the right side.

'You'd like me to collect?' said Joey.

'Please.'

'Right. I'll see the geezer and settle for what I can get. My end is twenty-five per cent. Agreed?'

Greenbaum shrugged his shoulders and spread out his hands.

'No haggling, Morrie. Is it a deal?'

'It's a deal, Joey.'

'Good. Now what can you tell me about this Gladwyn?'

Greenbaum pondered for a few moments.

'He ain't Jewish. A goy. Comes from the Midlands. Good-looking, smart. Cunning as a sewer rat.'

'Where can I find him?'

'His main shop. Just down the Garden, a few doors away. An office he's got, behind the shop. He's always there, nine to five-thirty.'

'Right. Let me out of this cage. I'll be in touch.'

Out in Hatton Garden, Joey made for the nearest pub. The public telephone was in a secluded corner. He dialled the office number and Marion came on the line.

'The Duchess there?' he said.

'Yes, Mr Bello,' came the reply.

'Get her to come to the phone.'

There was a brief pause before she came on the line.

'Yes, Joey,' she said.

'Bit of business,' said Joey. 'How long to get changed and look like a million dollars?'

'Fifteen minutes.'

'OK. Get Adgie to bring you to Finch's in High Holborn. He knows the place. I'll be waiting.'

The sun-tanned man inspecting the jewellery on display in the window of the shop in Hatton Garden gave every appearance of considerable wealth. The scar on his left cheek could have been the result of a motoring accident. The dark glasses might well have concealed some bruising. His companion, a ravishing and expensively-dressed blonde, moved the capacious Gucci handbag with its distinctive stripes from one shoulder to the other as she pointed out a solitaire diamond ring with a price tag of £25,000.

The door of the shop was locked, and the man pressed the bell push at the side. A well-dressed young man peered at the pair through the plate glass and, apparently satisfied that they were not the sort who robbed jewellery shops, opened the door to let them in.

'Good afternoon madame, sir,' he said.

He preceded them to the counter, which ran the length of the shop.

'May I see the solitaire? The one in the centre of the window,' said the girl. Her English was perfect with just a trace of accent.

'Certainly, madame.' The salesman was quick to retrieve the ring from the display. He laid it reverently on a square of black velvet on the counter. The girl picked it up and held it beneath a spotlight. Her companion gave the object no more than a cursory glance, but addressed a few words to her in a language that, to the young salesman, sounded utter gibberish. She replied in the same language.

She turned to the counter and inspected the ring more closely.

'Could we see something a little better?' she said.

'If you'll excuse me a moment, madame,' he said. 'I'll get Mr Gladwyn. I'm sure he'll be able to help you.' He disappeared towards the rear of the shop. There was the sound of a whispered conversation, then Mr Gladwyn made his personal appearance on the scene.

'Good afternoon madame, sir,' he said. 'I believe you would like to see some of our rarer pieces.'

'Please,' said the girl. 'This ring is very nice, but . . .'

'Would you come this way, please.'

Gladwyn leading the way, they passed to the rear of the shop. They came to a heavy oak door which Gladwyn opened, standing aside to allow the pair to enter. He followed them into the room and closed the door. He took a few paces towards his desk and the girl came up swiftly behind him. Her hands flew to his neck, she exerted a slight pressure with her fingers and he collapsed on to the heavy carpet.

'Well done, Duchess,' said Joey. He took off his dark glasses and put them in his pocket. 'How long before he comes round?'

'Any moment now,' said Francesca. As she uttered the words the man on the floor stirred and opened his eyes. He made an effort to scramble to his feet and managed to stand erect.

'All yours, Joey,' said Francesca.

Joey pounced. He grasped Gladwyn by the shoulders and flung him against the wall, followed him as he reeled away and shot a hard right to the pit of his stomach. The man sank to the floor, gasping for breath.

'Just stay where you are and listen to me,' said Joey. His

voice was hard and menacing. 'You owe a friend of mine a hundred grand. I've come to collect.'

Gladwyn was still in deep shock. He tried to stammer a few words.

'I'm not a patient man,' said Joey. 'Get up, go to that safe over there and get the money.'

Gladwyn staggered to his feet. As though hypnotised he moved slowly across the floor towards the safe. He turned to face his assailant.

'I – I – haven't got . . . that kind of money . . . here,' he gasped.

Joey moved swiftly towards him and put his face close to that of the terrified man.

'Shut up, you cunt,' he said. 'You're lighting out for Spain. That safe is stuffed with money. Now open the fucking thing or I'll tear your face off.'

The crudeness of the language coupled with Joey's menacing glare completed the demoralisation process. With shaking hands Gladwyn took out his keys and opened the safe. As Joey had rightly surmised, one of the shelves was packed with Treasury notes.

'A hundred and ten grand. Large denomination notes,' said Joey.

'You said . . . a hun . . .'

'A hundred grand. Collection fee ten per cent. Hand me your bag, Duchess.'

Joey rapidly packed the notes away as Gladwyn handed them to him. The task finished, Joey looked Gladwyn in the eye.

'I'm not going to give you a receipt and Morrie Greenbaum won't send you an account. If you're a clever boy you'll forget about this little episode. You've got plenty left. Go out to Spain and enjoy yourself. You might meet some friends of mine out there.'

He mentioned three names. Gladwyn went white and his jaw sagged.

'I'm in touch with them all the time. They'll let me know how you're getting on,' said Joey.

Gladwyn gave a despairing sigh. 'I won't say anything – to anybody,' he groaned.

'That's a good boy,' said Joey. 'Now tidy yourself up and see us out.'

Adgie was waiting a few yards down the street, chatting up a female traffic warden. He leapt to open the door of the Jaguar. Joey and Francesca collapsed into the comfort of the rear seats.

Francesca grinned. 'Tell me, Joey,' she said. 'Why didn't you take the lot?'

Joey grinned. 'Didn't you know? I'm going straight,' he said.

3. *The Killers*

The day of the party dawned bright and clear. Hyde Park was bathed in the June sunshine, couples strolled along the tree-fringed pathways or engaged in slightly more dubious activities on the grass and the gambolling dogs chased their own tails or each other with good-humoured impartiality. All was peaceful and serene.

Joey, in dressing-gown and slippers, reclined in an easy chair surrounded by the morning papers and looked out over what he thought of as his own special front garden. Two lines from a poem he had read at some time or another flashed through his mind, the plight of the poor prisoner "to whom the goodly light and air were banned and barred, forbidden fare". No more of that caper for me he said to himself, that's all behind me now. If I have to break the law to punish the lawbreakers, I'll be able to do it with a clear conscience.

His reflections were interrupted by a buzz on the internal telephone at his elbow. He picked up the receiver and Marion's voice came to him on the line.

'Good morning, Mr Bello. The caterers have arrived. Shall we go ahead as arranged?'

'Yes. Go right ahead. I'll be down shortly.'

He replaced the receiver and rose to his feet. With a last glance over his shoulder at the sunlit vista of his front garden, he strolled into the bedroom.

One hour later, immaculate in a dark blue hopsack, he went down the stairs to the main office which had been transformed into a fitting background for a small celebration. Harry, Fred and John had obeyed his instructions to the letter. The office equipment had been pushed back to the walls in the two rooms on the ground floor. In the front room a long trestle table had been set up, already covered with a snow-white cloth. In the other room Albert was presiding over the erection of a bar. The centres of the rooms were illuminated by spotlights, throwing the hooded office equipment into shadow.

Harry approached him as he stood surveying the transformation.

'Everything all right, Mr Bello?' he said. He was wearing a freshly cleaned uniform, as were his colleagues.

'Fine,' said Joey. 'Everything clear for tonight?'

'Yes, sir. Me, Fred and John sort of inconspicuous, keeping an eye on things. This floor and the basement open. No access to the upstairs part.'

'Right,' said Joey. 'I'm not expecting trouble, but you never know, so be prepared.'

He went down to the basement. The mat had been removed and a half-dozen small tables with attendant chairs occupied the vacant space. Spotlights on the walls threw a warm, rosy glow over the area. Marion, Helen and Jane sat at one of the tables, cups of tea before them. Joey grinned.

'Nothing like a cuppa before the performance,' he said. 'All under control?'

'Everything under control, Mr Bello,' said Helen. 'I think it's going to be a lovely party.'

'A lot depends on you three,' said Joey. 'I'll see you later.'

He mounted the stairs and went out through the front door. Adgie was adding a further shine to the already gleaming Jaguar.

'Come on, son,' said Joey. 'Got a bit of time to kill. Let's nip down to the Dale and have a few sherbets at the Warwick.'

It was half-past five when Joey got back to the house in Park Lane. Upstairs in his private rooms he dialled Francesca's number.

'Hello, Duchess,' he said in reply to her greeting. 'All set for the party?'

'Just getting the war-paint on,' she said. 'Be with you at seven-thirty. That be all right?'

'Excellent. The parents coming?'

'Certainly. They can't wait to meet you.'

'Let's hope they won't be disappointed,' he said. He replaced the receiver, went into the bathroom and ran a bath which he liberally anointed with Paco Rabane bath salts. Emerging from the bath, he took his time dressing. Black mohair trousers with a discreet silk stripe covering the outside seam, a silk shirt with a narrow black bow tie and a purple cummerbund around his waist. A single-breasted sharkskin jacket in white completed the picture. Joey regarded himself in the full-length mirror in the bedroom. He looked, and felt, like a million dollars. The little black box, his constant companion, fitted snugly into his trouser pocket.

Downstairs he made a quick tour of inspection. On the ground floor Kevin's minions had made a fine show. In the front room the buffet table was laden with a selection of cold meats and a bewildering array of appetising snacks, hot delicacies nestled in silver dishes over the flickering flames of spirit lamps and the rotund figure of the Bolinbroke's head chef, clad in immaculate whites, chef's hat worn jauntily over a ruddy bearded face, presided over the feast. Two white-jacketed waiters were in attendance, one at either end of the table.

In the back room the bar had been set up and was ready for business. The necks of a half-dozen magnums of Dom Perignon protruded from a large, ice-filled cooler; there was an abundance of wines and spirits and the highly-polished glasses shone in the rose-pink glow of the spotlights. Albert, as smart as paint in an obviously brand-new bar-tender's outfit, gave Joey a cheerful smile. He hauled an unlabelled bottle from a recess below the bar counter.

'The guv'nor sent a few bottles of the malt,' he said.

'They're welcome,' said Joey with an answering grin.

In the basement the three women were putting the finishing touches to the flower arrangements on the tables. Against the somewhat bizarre backdrop of parallel bars and other gymnasium gear the gilt chairs took on an added elegance. Soft music drifted from a speaker mounted in a corner of the room, where a small dance-floor had been laid. After a comprehensive glance round and an approving nod to his helpers, Joey mounted the steps to the hall.

Harry was on the point of opening the door to Francesca, whose image was projected sharply on the television screen. Joey went forward to welcome her.

'Duchess, you look wonderful,' he said.

Indeed she did. The plain black dress with a plunging neckline set off her golden hair. Her only jewellery consisted of a pair of drop earrings, single diamonds in a platinum setting.

'You don't look so bad yourself,' she said.

Further conversation was cut short by the arrival of Kevin O'Malley himself. Introduced to Francesca, he gave a low bow and touched her hand with his lips.

'This is a sight to gladden an old man's heart,' he said.

Francesca smiled and imitated his Irish accent.

'Now who's been kissing the Blarney stone!' she said.

O'Malley laughed delightedly. He turned to Joey.

'Came along early to see if my boys had done their stuff,' he said. 'How does it look?'

'Couldn't be better,' said Joey. 'Go and have a butcher's for yourself.'

'I'll do that,' said O'Malley, and took himself off in the general direction of the bar. Hardly had he done so than the guests began to flood in.

Among the first to arrive were Ace and his wife Belle, a startlingly beautiful West Indian. They were accompanied by a small man in a well-cut dinner jacket. Nicknamed the Weasel because he was always there or thereabouts without being noticed, he quickly merged into the background. Then followed a string of faces, old friends from the Dale and a few West End villains whom Joey knew and trusted. The champagne began to flow as the guests made themselves at home.

Albert worked overtime and the waiters rushed about, ensuring that nobody went hungry.

The party was moving into top gear when the important guests arrived. Joey and Francesca welcomed them in the hall.

There was a hint of mischief about the way in which Francesca performed the introductions.

'Joey, this is my father, Sir Alec Smithson-Wright QC,' she said. 'Daddy, my new partner, Joey Bello.'

Sir Alec had done his homework.

'Ah, yes, Bello,' he said. 'I remember. About ten years ago. Prosecuted you at the Old Bailey.'

Joey recalled the trial, the portly, silver-haired counsel for the prosecution whose impassioned plea for a maximum sentence cut no ice with the jury.

'I remember it well,' said Joey cheerfully. 'Made a proper bloody mess of it, didn't you?'

Concealing an imminent attack of the giggles, Francesca continued with the introduction.

'And this is my mother, Lady Fiona,' she said.

Lady Fiona was an older edition of her daughter, a handsome woman, well preserved with a trim figure encased in a Dior creation.

'Charmed,' said Joey. He took her hand and gently brushed it with his lips. Her ladyship was on the point of swooning. Here he was, a hero straight out of one of her romances, dark, penetrating eyes, deeply tanned, a scar down his left cheek – a duelling scar, perhaps – and a masterful air which he had just demonstrated in the battle of words with her husband. Weak at the knees, she stammered a few words in acknowledgement.

Francesca took command of the situation.

'Come on, Daddy, let me introduce you around,' she said. 'Joey, take care of Mummy, would you?'

Her father in tow, Francesca moved in the direction of the bar. Joey steered Lady Fiona towards a settee on to which she almost literally collapsed.

'What would you like to drink?' queried Joey. 'A glass of champagne, perhaps?'

Lady Fiona recovered her composure.

'Do you think your barman could mix me a champagne cocktail?' she said.

The party was going with a swing. The eminent QC had been lured into a corner by the Weasel and a well-known confidence trickster. They were deep in discussion, their tongues loosened by the liquor they had consumed. They were joined by Kevin, who brought an air of respectability and a bottle of the unlabelled single malt into the deliberations.

Some of the hounds from the Dale had gathered in a corner of the basement, where they swapped stories of their doings in and out of the nick. A few couples gyrated round the dance floor to the soft strains of Duke Ellington. Helen, Marion and Jane, granted permission by their slightly inebriated employer, began to circulate among the unattached males. Joey and Francesca flitted from group to group, exchanging banter and witticisms.

Lady Fiona had gravitated towards the handsome Ace and his beautiful wife. Their heads close together over a table in the basement, a bottle of brandy within easy reach, they gave vent to their feelings on a number of topics. They were on terms of first-name familiarity.

'Tell me, Fiona,' said Ace, 'why shouldn't my boys go to Eton? I put their names down when they were born. My father came here from Jamaica when he was ten. He was a British citizen. So am I.'

'I can see no reason why they shouldn't be accepted,' said Lady Fiona. Her speech was slightly slurred but she spoke with undoubted sincerity. 'After all, they wouldn't be the first black pupils there.'

She turned to Belle.

'What do you think, my dear?'

Belle arranged her features into an entrancing smile which did little more than show off her perfect teeth.

'I agree,' she said.

'By the way,' said her ladyship, 'I find Mr Bello quite interesting. Have you known him long?'

'Since I was a boy,' said Ace.

'Forgive me for asking, but what's his background? His parents, you know, that sort of thing?'

A flicker of a smile crossed Ace's handsome face.

'His mother must have been well-connected. When she married they had their reception in St James's Palace. Joey's mother told me they were waited on by royalty.'

'Really,' said Lady Fiona. 'I must have a long talk with Mr Bello. I find him quite fascinating.'

You're not the only one, thought Ace. Aloud he said, 'He's certainly that.'

Lady Fiona rose to her feet, swaying slightly.

'I think I should go and find him,' she said. 'Will you excuse me?'

'Your departure is our loss,' said Ace gallantly. He watched reflectively as her ladyship negotiated a course across the dance floor. He resumed his seat and turned to his wife.

'There goes a disturbed lady,' he said.

'I agree,' said Belle.

In the front room Joey was conferring with Adgie and the trio of security guards. The party was still going strong. At the table occupied by Kevin, Sir Alec, the Weasel and the con man, the malt had done its work. At the bar the indefatigable Albert was maintaining some sort of order as his customers broke into song. The smiling chef sipped at a glass of red wine.

'Don't let anybody drive home,' said Joey to Adgie. 'There's a fleet of limos waiting round the corner, on air call. You've got the number, Adgie?'

'I've got it.'

'Harry, Fred, John. Persuade their car keys out of them. Do it gently. Any trouble, get hold of me. I'll be around. Understood?'

The three men nodded.

'Right,' said Joey. 'I'll have a look round downstairs.'

In the hall he ran into Lady Fiona.

'Mr Bello,' she said. 'I've been looking for you.'

'You've found me, Lady Fiona,' he said. 'What can I do for you?'

She gave a ladylike hiccup. 'What goes on up these stairs?' she said. 'I was going up and one of your men stopped me.'

'My private quarters,' said Joey. 'No visitors allowed.'

Lady Fiona pouted. 'Not even little me?' she said.

Hello, thought Joey, what's the old trout up to. He came to a sudden decision.

'For you I'll make an exception,' he said. 'Come along.'

His hand under her elbow he piloted her up the stairs. The door opened as they approached and closed behind them as soon as they were inside. It was then that Lady Fiona pounced. She flung her arms round Joey's neck and made no secret of her intentions.

'Joey, Joey,' she panted. 'You lovely man. I want your body.'

Her breasts, surprisingly firm, were pressed against Joey's chest. She ground her hips against his. Joey felt himself respond. Her hand shot down to enfold his erection.

'Give it to me, Joey,' she hissed. 'I need it badly.'

Blimey, thought Joey, this is one for the book, but I'll give it a try. He hustled her into the front room, bent her over the back of a settee and flung her skirts over her head. She spread her legs in anticipation. The parting of the round, pink cheeks disclosed her sex. Lifting his cummerbund, Joey unzipped his trousers and let them fall round his ankles. His throbbing prick in his hand, he directed it between her thighs. He probed for a second then rammed himself brutally into her wet, warm channel. He began long slow strokes. Lady Fiona gave a muffled scream.

'Harder, harder. Talk dirty to me!'

Joey was beginning to enjoy himself. He lengthened the stroke.

'You've got . . . a lovely body,' he said, punctuating the

words with driving thrusts into the responsive body. 'You're a . . . lovely ride . . . I'm going to . . . fill you . . .'

She was ecstatic. 'I'm coming, I'm coming. Come with me. Oh, Joey, I love you.'

He felt the gathering explosion. As he ejaculated she closed her legs. His prick was held in a soft, tight grip as he drained himself into her. After a brief moment he began to withdraw. She screamed.

'No . . . no. Don't leave me.'

Joey laughed rather shakily. 'Sorry, milady. Nature calls.'

'Do it over me. Go on. I'd love it.'

I bet you would, thought Joey.

'No can do,' he said. He felt the contractions as she strained to retain his now limp weapon. She gave up and Joey withdrew. He pulled up his trousers, operated the zip and rearranged the cummerbund. Lady Fiona placed her hands on the back of the settee and levered herself to her feet. She was perfectly composed.

'Shall we join the others?' said Joey.

Lady Fiona smiled. 'I'll visit the bathroom first. You are certainly a very virile man, Joey. My cup is filled to overflowing.'

Joey followed her into the bathroom. He took a long and leisurely pee as Lady Fiona perched herself on the bidet and caressed her genitalia with soapy hands. Joey was the first to emerge. He waited in the hall, where he was shortly joined by the lady. She caressed his arm.

'What about a little quickie before we go down,' she said.

'Another time, milady,' said Joey.

Lady Fiona leading the way, they came into the front room. The pace of the party was slackening, although the chef was still serving food to the guests who had decided to come back for a second helping. With a smile Joey excused himself and wandered into the back room, which was by now exclusively male. Kevin was holding forth on the subject of an Irish-bred filly which was going to be the horse of the century. Good old Kevin, thought Joey, he'll be holding a bloodstock sale before long.

At the bar Albert was serving drinks to three familiar faces who waved to him in greeting. As he gave them a wave in return, they were joined by a frizzy-haired blonde who looked as though she had been poured into her dress and somebody had forgotten to say when. Joey recognised her instantly as he remembered the occasion when he had last seen her – a hugely successful party at J. Arthurs night-club in Catford, held to celebrate the closing of the pantomime 'Puss in Boots' at the local theatre.

Joey was at the time managing the club, and had been approached by television personality Jeremy Beadle to organise the party. It all came back to him in a flood of remembrance, perky little Bonnie Langford, the irrepressible Lulu, the imposing figure of George Sewell and Henry McGee, who could be relied upon to light up a party anytime and anywhere as he did so often on the Benny Hill show.

As the festivities had come to a close Joey had stood with a small group near the bar. Jeremy Beadle came up to him.

'Joey,' he said. 'You've done a fine job. Pass on my thanks to your staff. I've put a little something over the bar for them.'

'Much appreciated, Jeremy,' said Joey.

Beadle drew Joey to one side. 'Isn't that Eddie Richardson there?' he said.

'That's right,' said Joey. 'He owns the place.'

'I'd like to meet him.'

'No sweat,' said Joey. He turned to Eddie who was standing behind him.

'Eddie,' he said. 'I'd like you to meet Jeremy Beadle.'

Eddie smiled. 'I recognised you,' he said.

The two men shook hands. 'I recognised you, too,' said Jeremy Beadle.

Joey was brought back into the present by a light tap on his shoulder. He turned sharply, to find himself confronted by a smiling Francesca.

'Hello, Duchess,' he said. 'Enjoying the celebrations?'

'Never had a better time in my life,' she said. 'I think the parents have had enough though. I'll see them home and then it's beddy-byes for me. See you Monday?'

'I'll be here,' said Joey.

The last of the revellers departed as dawn began to light the sky. Kevin brought up the rear as the ever-present Adgie ushered the guests to the waiting limousines.

'Joey, me boy,' he said, 'if it goes as well as it's started, you'll be on the way to a fortune.'

'It will and I am,' said Joey succinctly.

Indoors the staff had already embarked on the clean-up operation. With 'goodnights' all round, Joey mounted the stairs to his private sanctum.

The four men sitting round the table in the restaurant of the Ritz Hotel could have been mistaken for wealthy businessmen celebrating a successful merger over dinner. Soberly dressed in well-cut lounge suits, their jewellery discreet but expensive, they talked in low voices against the soft background music of muted violins.

The host, Eddie Richardson, sat facing the room. On his left was the corpulent figure of his brother-in-law, known to his friends and acquaintances as Italian Paul, a man who loved his food and made no secret of the fact. Next to him sat Roy Hall, Eddie's lifelong friend, a short, powerfully-built man who looked as fit as a regiment of Marines, despite a long medical history of heart trouble. Joey made up the fourth member of the quartet.

They studied the menu as they sipped their aperitifs.

'They do a good set meal,' said Eddie. 'How about it?'

'Not bleeding likely,' said Paul. 'Not enough to feed a starving gnat.' He turned to Joey. 'Order what you like, my son. You're not in the nick now.'

'Tell me something I don't know,' said Joey.

The waiter came up to take their order. Eddie, who watched his diet, selected a simple starter followed by a rare sirloin steak. Roy followed his example. Joey went for the goujons of sole and the tournedos Rossini.

The waiter turned to Paul. 'And for you, sir?' he said.

Paul had studied the menu with great care. He pointed to three items. He said, 'I'll have double portions of this – and this – and this. After that I'd like a selection from the hors d'oeuvre trolley.'

The waiter kept a straight face. 'And to follow, sir?'

'A large rump steak. Some fresh vegetables on the side and a green salad.'

The waiter turned to Eddie. 'I'll send the wine waiter,' he said.

The sommelier duly presented himself, handing the wine list to Eddie. A discriminating connoisseur of the best vintages, Eddie ordered wine to match the food they were about to eat. As the sommelier left the table Joey turned to Roy.

'Remember that night at Blazes' in Windsor?' he said.

'Will I ever forget it,' Roy replied. 'I was well and truly schickered.'

'You frightened the life out of Joe Longthorne,' said Joey. 'Diving into the pool at his house. Freezing cold it was. You could have snuffed it.'

Roy laughed. 'Take more than that to see me off,' he said.

Over the excellent food the conversation was confined to generalities. Paul took little part in the exchange of anecdotes about old friends and past adventures. He applied himself to demolishing the succession of dishes that appeared before him. When the trolley laden with appetising hors d'oeuvres was wheeled to the table, Paul let himself go.

'God bless your little tum,' said Eddie. Paul, his mouth stuffed with delicacies, merely grunted.

As the four friends ate, drank and made merry, by coincidence another meeting was taking place within a hundred yards of the Ritz. In the lounge of the gentlemen's club in St James's, Matthew Gill was in close conversation with Commander Finch. Though they spoke in low tones, it was obvious that their discussion was anything but friendly.

Finch was speaking. 'Now look here, Gill,' he said. 'For Christ's sake get off my back. I'm doing my best . . .'

'And your best isn't good enough,' interjected Gill. 'I'm staggered. Here you are, a Commander in the Metropolitan Police, and you tell me that you're defeated by a common criminal. What the hell's the matter with you?'

'How many times do I have to tell you that Bello is no common criminal,' said Finch. 'Down in the Dale they call him a one-man army. His father was a bare-knuckle fighter. Old George Bello would take on four fights a day at half-a-dollar a time. They're a fighting family. Kick one and the rest limp.'

'Spare me the hearts and flowers,' said Gill. 'Your lot managed to dispose of those strumpets we used at the orgies. What's the difference?'

'Don't go too far,' said Finch. 'First of all I had nothing to do with those murders. That's down to Leon the ponce.'

'Who happens to be conveniently dead,' said Gill.

'That's history. Now shut up and listen to me. Bello's teamed up with Francesca Smithson-Wright. They're running a private investigation racket. She can open a lot of doors for him. He's not short of cash. He's taken a place in Park Lane. Spent a small fortune on turning it into a fortress. Her father's a QC who'll be a judge one of these days. Now do you see what I'm up against?'

Gill sank back in his chair. There was silence as he considered the implications of Finch's outburst, and he realised for the first time that the Commander was reaching the end of his tether.

'All right, Finch,' he said. 'This isn't the time for self-pity. Something positive has to be done, and you're the only man who can do it. Let's have some concrete proposals. And don't forget, by the way, that we have the big battalions on our side.'

'If it comes to the point where we have to call up the big battalions, that's when I'm finished,' said Finch. 'However big I am, I can always be brought down. Look at what happened to Virgo and the others. The Rubber Heels are breathing down my neck.'

'Rubber Heels?' said Gill. 'Who are they?'

'The internal investigation department at the Yard. They're poking their noses into my affairs.'

'Why?' asked Gill. 'You're supposed to be above suspicion.'

'Nobody's above suspicion at the Yard. It's a bloody jungle. If the press isn't sniping at us then the Commissioner is on our backs moaning about the rise in the crime rate. We're on a hiding to nothing.'

'That's defeatist talk, Finch,' said Gill. 'Look at the situation realistically. The only fly in the ointment is Bello. Get him out of the way and the rest is plain sailing and you've nothing to fear. We have some very good friends in high places. They can take care of the law because they are the law. Who the hell cares about scrubby little policemen digging up dirt. Where's their evidence?'

'If they get hold of those tapes that Bello copied they'll have more than enough to send you, me and a lot of others into the boob for a very long time . . .'

'Which is where we came in,' said Gill. 'Bello's got to be dead. Come on, man. Pull yourself together. You've got the contacts. You've only to snap your fingers and Bello will be out of the picture for good.'

'It won't be easy,' said Finch.

Gill changed his tactics. His experience in the psychiatric field had taught him that hard words, if they were to be effective, should be followed by a pat on the back. Privately he had little time for Finch who, in his opinion, was a prick who deserved no consideration whatsoever. There flashed across his mind a scene from one of the videotapes, a naked Finch lying on his back caressing the ample breasts of an equally naked woman who was sucking at his penis in a vain endeavour to restore it to an erect position.

Repressing a smile, Gill adopted his bedside manner. Now was the time for cajolery. He spoke quietly and gently.

'You're a highly intelligent fellow, Finch. A man who attains your position in the finest police force in the world doesn't get to that position by chance. Don't let yourself be stampeded by fears of what may happen. See the situation objectively and take what you know to be the right course of action.'

Finch rubbed his chin reflectively. After all, he thought, there was a lot in what Gill had said. Why should he worry about a toerag like Bello. It was quite true that he need only snap his fingers and the man would be disposed of once and for all. A plan began to form in his mind.

'You're right, Gill,' he said. 'No need for panic stations. Leave it to me.'

Gill smiled. His stratagem had worked, and he now knew for certain that the pig-headed man sitting opposite him would go all out to ensure Bello's elimination.

'I must be off now,' he said. 'Let's hope you'll have good news for me the next time we meet.'

Finch's face took on what was known to his subordinates at the Yard as the Goldfinch glare, a grim-jawed determined expression befitting a Commander who knew how to command.

'I'll be in touch,' he said.

After Gill had made his exit, Finch remained seated for a while.

Despite his brave words he was under no illusions as to the task which faced him. Everything he knew about Bello pointed to the fact that he would be dealing with a resourceful character who knew all the tricks of the trade, and a few more besides. He rose from his chair and went into the lobby of the club. There he made a short telephone call from the coin box.

At the porter's desk he left a message for his driver that his services would not be required again that evening. Passing rapidly through a short passage to the kitchens, he left via the tradesmen's door. Walking through to Jermyn Street, he hailed a taxi.

'Take me to Cable Street,' he said. 'I'll tell you where to drop me.'

The square mile of the City of London is the greatest casino in the world. Within its boundaries sophisticated gambling has become an almost precise science, with billions of pounds changing hands daily in complicated financial transactions manipulated by gentlemen who would raise their hands in horror were they accused of improper or illegal activities.

To the east of the Tower of London lies a sharply contrasting area where outright criminality is a way of life for a considerable proportion of its residents. Where Cable Street has its beginnings the traveller is plunged into the dark and mysterious hinterland of Whitechapel, where decaying buildings are largely occupied by immigrants of varying shades of colour ranging from light brown to the deepest black, where every variety of crime from mugging to murder is a daily commonplace and where civilisation fights a losing battle against the anarchy of violence.

The taxi had travelled a hundred yards or so along Cable Street. Finch rapped on the window, and the cab slid to a stop. Alighting from the vehicle, Finch paid off the driver and stood for a while on the pavement until the glowing tail lights disappeared in the darkness. He began to walk in an easterly direction and came to a dimly-lit side street into which he turned after a comprehensive look round the immediate vicinity.

The man driving the nondescript Ford saloon, who had followed Finch's cab from Jermyn Street, drew up at the kerb. The occupant got out and moved swiftly and silently to the corner of the street into which Finch had turned. He was just in time to see that his quarry had halted outside a derelict-looking house and was in the act of knocking on the door. Withdrawing into a convenient doorway, he spoke softly into the walkie-talkie set concealed beneath his jacket.

'Subject entering 12 Union Street off Cable Street. Over.'

'Message acknowledged,' said the disembodied voice. 'Maintain surveillance and report. Over and out.'

As the watcher returned to his car Finch was being admitted into the house.

The hallway was in almost total darkness, but Finch, who was no stranger to the place, walked purposefully down the passage to where a strip of light showed the entrance to the room at the rear. He pushed the door open and, closely followed by the man who had let him in, stood for a moment surveying the scene before him.

By no stretch of the imagination could it be described as salubrious. The room was fairly large. The table in the centre was a clutter of empty bottles and dirty glasses. Over in a corner stood a cooker flanked by a sink which was piled with unwashed plates and cooking utensils. A single unshaded electric light was the sole illumination. The air was thick with tobacco smoke.

Sitting in chairs near the table were two of the men who had been called to the meeting. Ian James, known throughout the underworld as Basher, was a massive brute who, standing erect, topped the six foot four mark. His reputation was fearsome. He had been known to take on gangs of heavies bent on his destruction, beat them into a pulp and walk away from the scene completely undamaged.

His companion, in complete contrast, was small and slim, a wiry Spaniard whose reputation had been built on his skill with the knife, a seven inch blade which was his constant companion. The stories about him were legion. One in particular concerned the fate of a grass. The police surgeon who had carried out the post mortem had expressed his admiration of the skill with which the dissection of the corpse had been carried out. 'It must have been a tricky job,' he said. 'Particularly since the victim was most probably alive at the time.' On police records he appeared as Pedro Ramirez. In the underworld he was famous as Spanish Pete.

The third member of the firm came from behind the

Commander into the circle of light thrown by the single bulb. Tall, thin to the point of emaciation, his sunken eyes and cadaverous cheeks, together with an unusual pallor, marked him out as a drug addict. Long hair flowed over his shoulders and he was dressed habitually in filthy denim. He was known as Hippie Palmer.

As Finch drew up a chair and seated himself, Hippie did likewise. Basher James was the first to break the silence.

'What's the trouble, guv'nor?' he said.

Finch gave the three men the benefit of the Goldfinch glare. He knew that he was dealing with hard men and he selected his words carefully, making sure that they understood exactly what he meant.

'Say "sir" when you talk to me, James,' he said. 'Cut out the "guv'nor" shit. And you, Palmer, take that fucking grin off your face.' To Pedro, who was cleaning his nails with his knife, he said, 'Put that fucking toothpick away and sit up straight when I'm talking to you.'

They were killers, men who had scant regard for the sanctity of human life, but they reacted immediately to Finch's attack. Hippie's face took on a serious look, Basher was suitably brought to order and Spanish Pete put away the chiv and sat bolt upright.

Finch continued the verbal attack.

'I don't have any trouble,' he said. 'You're the ones with grief. Just remember that when I tell you what I want done.'

Finch was an old-fashioned copper who believed in tried and tested methods. When dealing with villains the first step was to dominate the situation, then put on the frighteners and follow this with specific instructions as to what was to be done linked with a hint about the dire consequences which would follow failure to deliver the goods. He used strong language in the belief that it gave emphasis to what he had to say.

His audience was in no position to argue. They were fully aware that Finch could put them away for the rest of their natural lives. They listened to him intently.

'Some months ago,' said Finch, 'you were given a contract on Joey Bello. You reported to me that he had been killed in a car crash. Right?'

Hippie cleared his throat as a prelude to speech.

'Don't bother to make excuses,' Finch went on. 'And don't tell me any more fucking lies. Bello is alive and well and living in Park Lane. He's started a private enquiry racket. He's gone into partnership with a young society woman who is very well-connected. He has plenty of cash.'

Finch drew a bulky envelope from his pocket and threw it on the table.

'There's all the information you will need. Photos of the house in Park Lane. Bello and his partner, his staff and his driver. His car is a black Jaguar V12.'

Finch got up from his chair. The others also rose and stood to semi-attention.

'I don't want to hear from you again until Bello is dead,' said Finch. 'I'll see myself out.'

As the Commander left, the three men resumed their seats. Hippie rubbed his chin reflectively.

'It isn't going to be easy,' he said.

'Too fucking right,' said Basher. 'Better get your thinking cap on, Hippie.'

The little Spaniard said nothing. He reached into his pocket, drew out his blade and continued the manicure that Finch had interrupted.

Finch came out into Union Street, turned at the corner and walked rapidly westwards. At the junction of Leman Street and Royal Mint Street he hailed a prowling cab. The watcher, who had followed at a discreet distance, spoke softly into the microphone.

'Subject in taxi headed west,' he said.

'Maintain surveillance and report,' said the voice. 'You will be relieved in one hour.'

4. *The Video Pirates*

Francesca was doing a work-out in the basement gym. Completely naked save for a pair of tiny briefs, she went into a routine on the parallel bars. Her body glistened with sweat which ran in small rivulets between her taut breasts. As she finished the routine with a perfect somersault onto the mat, Joey entered. She waved a greeting.

'Morning, Duchess,' said Joey. He surveyed her dispassionately. 'Doing too much with the weights,' he said. 'Watch it, or you'll get muscle-bound.'

He disappeared into the shower room, emerging a few moments later in shorts and singlet. Without a glance at his partner, he rapidly executed a hundred press-ups, then moved to the spring bag, beating a well-timed tattoo for six minutes. Transferring his attention to the heavy bag, he thumped away for a further six minutes, ending with a mighty right hook which almost tore the bag from its moorings. Francesca had meanwhile suspended operations, sitting cross-legged on the mat.

'Very impressive,' she said as Joey wiped the sweat from his face and arms. 'Now, how about teaching me some of the tricks of the trade?'

'Sure,' said Joey. He dropped the towel and moved in towards her. The words were hardly out of his mouth when she launched a savage drop-kick at his head which, had it landed, would have put him out for the count. As it was, Joey moved easily to one side and the kick passed over his shoulder. Blimey, thought Joey, she's being serious, and pivoted on his right foot as Francesca cartwheeled to come up behind him poised for a rabbit chop at his neck. As it was, Joey was facing her before she delivered the blow. His left arm around her neck, Joey drew her close to him as he shot a shattering right hook into her solar plexus. Every ounce of breath expelled from her lungs, Francesca collapsed on hands and knees.

For a full five seconds Joey stood and watched her as she struggled to regain her breath, finally slipping his hands beneath her arms and helping her to her feet.

'You've been on the deck long enough for me to kick your ribs in and stamp your face flat,' said Joey. 'That would have made you a hospital case. If I'd wanted to put you in the mortuary I'd have kicked you here . . .' He laid a finger gently against her temple.

Francesca began to breathe more easily.

'Point taken,' she said.

'What you've got to remember,' said Joey, 'is that the first thing to do is to put the other fellow on the floor. All this dancing about and arm waving is all right for TV and the films. It doesn't work that way when you're facing a hard case who is going to chop you up into little pieces. Don't worry. A few more lessons and you'll be ready for the big league.'

'Can't wait,' she said. 'Only next time do me a favour.'

'Anything to oblige,' said Joey. 'What's the favour, Duchess?'

'Just pull your punches.'

'Will do. Now I'm going to take a shower and have a cup of coffee upstairs. Join me?'

'Right with you.'

In the upstairs sitting room the coffee pot and cups were already on the table when Francesca made her appearance. Lying beside the tray was a peculiar object which she picked up and examined closely.

'What's this?' she asked.

'That, Duchess, is a knuckle-duster,' said Joey. 'You put your fingers through the four holes there, rest the curved part in your palm and you've got an iron fist.'

Francesca tried it out for size.

'Bit big for you,' said Joey. 'I'll get you a smaller model.'

'I've got it. My tiny hands are a bit fragile for the big punch. With this I can break ribs.'

'Right,' said Joey. 'You can also break jaws. Wait until the geezer opens his mouth then stick one on the angle of the jaw. He'll be taking his food through straws for a month.'

Francesca laughed. 'Any more cute tricks?' she said.

Joey reached under the table and pulled out a pair of shoes, which Francesca examined minutely.

'Hm. Very nice. Made by Lobb, I see. Must have cost a fair bit.'

Joey took the shoes from her and picked up a spoon with which he rapped the toes. There was a metallic ring.

'Steel caps,' said Joey. 'Guaranteed to produce the maximum damage in the shortest time. Let me have a couple of pairs of your shoes and I'll have them converted. Just in case.'

'I'll do that little thing,' she said. She sipped her coffee thoughtfully, then gave Joey a level glance. 'I'd like to ask you a question. I want an honest answer.'

'Ask away,' said Joey.

'Why haven't you made a pass at me?'

'I thought you would have known the reason.'

'Answer the question, Joey,' she said.

'All right. I'll be blunt. If I want a fuckpiece I'll get one. There's plenty of it about. You're not in that category. Satisfied?'

'Not completely. Elaborate, will you?'

'You want me to?'

'Please.'

'Right. I've sussed you out. You're a very private person. Your body is yours and you don't intend to let some bloke stick his cock into you because he says he loves you. My guess is that you're a virgin and that you mean to stay that way.'

Francesca smiled. 'You're a very perceptive person, Joey. Can I let my hair down? No secrets?'

'Feel free,' said Joey.

'I've never talked to anybody about this,' she said. 'Since I was a kid the boys have always chased me. I was fifteen when some macho idiot who thought he was God's gift to women decided that he wasn't going to take no for an answer. I half-killed him.'

'Good for you, Duchess,' said Joey.

She carried on as though there had been no interruption.

'They call it making love. How the hell do you make love? Is it a manufactured article? Fucking, screwing, congress, copulation, bonking, that's all it is. Why should I lie on my back and let some all-conquering male violate my body as he pumps away using me to sell his imagination back to himself. Not on your fucking Nellie.'

'Bravo, Duchess!' said Joey.

Francesca laughed. 'Now let me have your views on the subject,' she said.

'They're simple. I never think with my bollocks. I get into an emotional relationship with you and we might as well pack it in. We can't go into a caper with me feeling all protective about you. That way we're both vulnerable.'

'So now we know where we stand,' she said.

'That's right, Duchess. Now we know where we stand.'

Francesca was about to make some rejoinder when the internal phone buzzed. Joey reached over and picked up the handset.

'Yes.'

Marion's voice came on the line. 'A call from Sir Frederick Morton, Mr Bello,' she said.

'You've checked it out?'

'Usual check. Asked for a number, said you'd ring back in five minutes. The number's genuine.'

'Who's this Morton fellow?'

'He's on computer. Chairman and Managing Director of Intervideo plc. Producers of video cassettes for the retail market. Pound shares quoted today at eight forty-nine. Annual turnover three billion . . .'

'That's enough. Get him on the phone. Get out a

comprehensive memo on the company and have it ready for me in fifteen minutes.'

Joey replaced the receiver.

'What was all that about?' asked Francesca.

'Looks like we're in business. Chap called Sir Frederick Morton wants to talk to me. Know him?'

'Indeed I do. Friend of Daddy's. Pretentious little shit. Daddy led for the prosecution in a couple of cases. Breach of copyright. Wonder what he wants?'

'We'll soon find out,' said Joey. As he spoke the phone buzzed. He picked up the receiver, and a voice which sounded as though it was being strained through hot mashed potatoes came over the line.

'Bello? Sir Frederick Morton here. I have a proposition for you. When can we meet?'

'No time like the present, Sir Frederick. Your office. Shall we say twelve-thirty?'

'Good.' The line went dead.

'So that was Sir Frederick,' said Francesca. 'Man of few words.'

'I've got a meet with him. Twelve thirty at his office. I'd like you to come along.'

'Of course. What's the time now?'

Joey glanced at his watch. 'Plenty of time. It's eleven o'clock. Finish your coffee, then we'll go down and see what Marion has dug up.'

The information contained in the single sheet of typescript which Marion had prepared was packed with facts. A breakdown on Intervideo's latest returns under the provisions of the Companies Act was followed by extracts of Press reports dealing with a number of actions in the High Court against what were referred to as 'video pirates'. The purpose of Morton's phone call was now quite plain. He was suffering from the unwelcome attentions of the pirates and intended to enlist the services of J. Bello Investigations in ridding himself of the nuisance.

Scanning the list of actions, Joey's eye was caught by a

report that four million pounds had been awarded in damages against John Barnham and Neil Rivers, who had pleaded guilty to copying films at premises in Brentford. At the end of the news item appeared a single illuminating sentence. 'The two men are unlikely to be able to pay'. Joey chuckled. That was Johnny Barnham all over. The mention of the name took him back to the time when he was minding World Welterweight Champion Sugar Ray Leonard, in London to attend a boxing show in aid of the Bud Flanagan Leukaemia Fund.

The occasion was a gathering at the Thomas à Beckett pub in the Old Kent Road. It started out as a press party, but news of the event leaked out and more than two thousand people descended on the place. Celebrities were there in force. Joey noticed among them Errol Christie and his manager Bert McCarthy, the silver-haired Ted 'Kid' Lewis, Dave Boy Green and a host of others. Actors Edward Fox and Alan Lake, husband of Diana Dors, were in the crowd. Eddie Richardson was also present, as were a number of well-known faces from Stepney and Whitechapel.

Sugar Ray was three hours late in arriving at the venue. Joey remembered how he and his young assistant had to fight their way through the crowd in order to deliver their charge safely, how Leonard had put on an electrifying exhibition of sparring, skipping and a work out on the heavy bag and the final event when Sugar Ray signed hundreds of autographs for his adoring fans.

The voice at his elbow said, 'Mind if I have a look at that bundle of bumph?'

'Sorry, Duchess,' said Joey. 'I was miles away. Here you are.'

He handed the breakdown to Francesca, who read it through rapidly.

'Looks like we have a nice little tickle here,' she said.

'Tell me about this Morton fellow,' said Joey.

'Well, he's middle-fifties, short, fat, wears a toupee. A bit of an idiot in some respects but as cunning as a bag of rats when it comes to business. That's my personal opinion.'

'Good enough. Can you climb into your business gear and be back here by twelve?'

'No trouble. See you,' she said.

Joey went through to the rear office. Helen looked up as he entered.

'Open up a file on Intervideo plc. Chairman and Managing Director Sir Frederick Morton. Get all the relevant details from Marion. OK?'

'Right, Mr Bello.'

At twelve-thirty precisely Francesca and Joey were ushered into the sumptuous office of the Chairman and Managing Director of Intervideo plc. As they entered, Joey pressed the button on the small recorder in his inside pocket, a gesture unnoticed by the short, fat man who swooped on Francesca, seizing both her hands in greeting.

'My dear Francesca,' he burbled, 'how nice to see you. You're looking more beautiful than ever . . .'

Francesca brusquely interrupted the insincere flow of compliments.

'This is my partner, Mr Joey Bello,' she said. Morton shot a glance in Joey's direction but did not offer his hand.

'Please sit down,' he said, waving towards two comfortable armchairs as he retired behind an ornate desk and seated himself in a chair which had obviously been built up to conceal his lack of stature. 'Now, can I offer you tea or coffee – or perhaps something stronger?'

'Nothing for me, thank you,' said Francesca. Joey shook his head and spoke for the first time.

'Shall we get down to business,' he said.

Slightly disconcerted by the direct approach, Morton put the tips of his fingers together and gave Joey what he imagined to be a penetrating glance which lasted all of five seconds. Then, as though he were addressing a board meeting, he launched into what was patently a prepared speech.

'Well now, Bello,' he began, 'I don't know how much you know about the video business . . .?'

He paused. Joey remained impassive.

Morton went on. 'We are a large public company with a quite considerable turnover manufacturing video cassettes for the retail market. Over the years we have sustained losses due to the activities of what we call video pirates who obtain advance copies of films, of which we own the distribution rights, and flood the market with cheap copies. Recently the activities of these pirates have been stepped up and, as the largest manufacturer in the trade, we have decided to take some positive action. My friend Sir Alec, whom I believe you have met, mentioned that you might be of some assistance to us being, as it were -ah – not unacquainted with the criminal community . . .'

'You mean set a thief to catch a thief. I've heard that before,' said Joey. 'Let's cut the cackle.' Deliberately omitting the man's title, he went on.

'What do you estimate your losses have been over, say, the past two years, Morton?'

Morton waved a hand airily. 'Not very large,' he said, 'but we feel we owe it to our shareholders to do something about it.'

Owe it to your shareholders, you fat little sod, thought Joey, you're more concerned with lining your pockets. Aloud he said, 'What do you estimate your losses at over the past couple of years?'

'As I told you, not very large . . .'

'In figures?'

'Let's say about a hundred thousand.'

'You're a bloody little liar,' said Joey calmly. 'According to your trade association, the Federation Against Copyright Theft, the figure is around twenty million. If we take on the job of providing evidence leading to prosecution and conviction our terms are one hundred thousand pounds down and a further four hundred thousand on conviction. Plus expenses, of course. Let us have your acceptance together with your cheque for a hundred grand and we'll go to work. In the event we fail to deliver the goods its cost you a hundred grand.'

The little man spluttered. 'It's preposterous. Highway robbery . . .'

'Those are the terms. Take them or leave them,' said Joey. 'Come on, Duchess. We've got work to do.'

Outside the building Francesca roared with laughter.

'You cheeky bastard,' she said. 'You'll never get away with it.'

'Wait and see,' said Joey. 'It works at all levels. Put 'em on the deck, kick shit out of them and you get a result.'

Adgie popped up out of nowhere.

'The car's just round the corner, sir,' he said. 'I'll have it here in half a jiffy.'

He trotted away. Joey turned to Francesca.

'I think we deserve a nice little lunch,' he said.

'You deserve something for your bloody cheek,' she replied.

Over lunch at the Inn on the Park they discussed the broad outlines of a plan of action in the event that Morton accepted the proposition which had been put to him.

'As I see it,' said Joey, 'this caper has been going on for some considerable time and up to now Intervideo hasn't been able to put a stop to it. Morton's desperate, and desperate men grasp at straws. Four hundred grand's nothing to him. That doesn't mean he won't try to get what he wants as cheaply as he can – and I bet he's tried that too. This isn't a job for seedy ex-coppers working out of a back room in a Soho side street.'

'So how do you propose to tackle it?' said Francesca. 'These pirates aren't a gang of amateurs running off a few odd copies of films in a lock-up garage. It must be a big operation with plenty of money behind it – and plenty of muscle too.'

'So it's up to us to find out the strength of it and take the necessary steps.'

'You're not worried? I mean some of your old mates might be involved.'

'That's their look-out. The word's gone out that I'm in the

private eye business, and if they want to go against me they'll have to take the consequences. Makes no odds to me.'

'Don't forget you've got enemies,' she said. 'They might throw a spanner in the works.'

'I haven't forgotten. They'll come at me sooner or later and I'll be ready. So will you – partner.'

'Can't wait. This lazing about in posh hotels is killing me. Let's have some action.'

Joey smiled grimly. 'If I'm any judge we'll see plenty of that in the very near future.'

They were back in the office at half-past three. The lunch, though excellent, had been frugal and they had drunk only Perrier water. They went into the front office, where Joey handed the miniature tape recorder to Marion.

'Get this transcribed,' he said. 'Head it "Meeting with Sir Frederick Morton, Intervideo Offices", commencing twelve-thirty pip emma, today's date. Give it to Helen for the Intervideo file.'

'Yes, Mr Bello,' she said. 'Anything else?'

'Some tea upstairs. Come on, Duchess. We'll continue our chat over a cuppa.'

The letter arrived by special messenger at four o'clock. It was brought to the upstairs rooms by Helen. She handed it to Joey, who lost no time in opening it and extracting the contents, which consisted of a single sheet of paper and a cheque. He read the short letter, inspected the cheque then passed the two documents to Francesca. He turned to Helen.

'Messenger still waiting?' he said.

'Yes, Mr Bello.'

'Ring down and tell Marion to let him go.'

Helen picked up the internal phone and murmured a few words. Francesca finished her reading, passed the letter and cheque back to Joey and burst into a roar of laughter.

'Proposition accepted unconditionally. Cheque for one

hundred thousand pounds enclosed,' she quoted. 'Joey Bello, you are one brilliant bastard. You've got the pompous little prat over a barrel.'

Joey put on a mock-Oxford accent. 'Your comment is unladylike but accurate, my dear Duchess,' he said.

He gave the letter and cheque to Helen. 'Pay the money into the number one account. Send an acknowledgement and our standard form of contract to Morton. Mark it personal and private. Details of my verbal offer on the tape Marion gave you. Get an authenticated voice print from Morton. Usual procedure. Personal phone call, voice print the conversation, attested by two witnesses, dated and timed. All clear?'

'Quite clear, Mr Bello,' she said. She turned and left the room.

'Now, Duchess,' said Joey, 'we plan the operation and get a team together. I'm going to bring Ace in on this. We shall need an electronics man and quite a number of men and women for detailed surveillance. Just a minute.'

He picked up the internal phone. 'Marion,' he said. 'Get hold of Ace Johnson. Tell him I want to see him here as soon as possible. Give me a buzz back and tell me when to expect him.'

'Hang about,' said Francesca. 'Where do I come in?'

'This is where you come in, Duchess. You and me will be at the sharp end. These pirates aren't going to throw their hands up and cough the lot without a fight. If there's any rough stuff we take care of it. There's an old saying, if you want a job done properly, do it yourself.'

'Now you're talking,' said Francesca. 'Carry on.'

'We'll be in sole charge. Work out the tactics, brief the teams. Anything goes wrong we jump in pronto and put it right. Agreed?'

'Agreed.'

There was a buzz from the internal phone. Marion was on the line.

'I've spoken to Mr Johnson,' she said. 'He's on his way, and will be with you in fifteen minutes.'

'Thanks,' said Joey. He replaced the receiver.

'Right. I've got a little present for you, Duchess,' he said. He went over to an occasional table against the wall and pulled open one of the drawers, taking out a pair of objects which Francesca recognised as smaller editions of the knuckle-dusters she had seen that morning.

'Try these on for size,' he said. 'Fingers through the holes. Get that curved bit hard against the heel of the hand. Take a firm grip and don't relax it when you go into action. Let the metal do the work.'

Francesca stood relaxed, arms hanging down, her small fists turned into deadly weapons.

'Comfy?' asked Joey.

'Very,' she replied.

'Good. When you go in, aim for the solar plexus, left or right hand, makes no difference. If you're on target you'll paralyse the geezer at the receiving end. A bit off target and he collects a couple of broken ribs. Whichever way, he goes down. That's when you introduce him to your specialist shoemakers.'

Francesca giggled and, like a child with a new toy, danced around the room, shooting out short lefts and rights. As she moved closer to Joey, he held up a warning hand.

'Whatever you're thinking of, don't do it,' he said. 'I know the answer to brass knuckles too.'

Francesca gave a shamefaced grin. 'Just thought I might try them out,' she said.

'You'll have plenty of opportunity for that in the near future if I'm any judge,' said Joey.

At that moment the arrival of Ace was announced.

'Send him up,' said Joey. He moved into the hall, the door swung open and Ace bounced in. In response to Joey's gesture he made his way into the room overlooking the Park, where he greeted Francesca with his usual exuberance. He stood for a moment looking out of the window.

'Nice front garden,' he observed.

'Yeah,' Joey paused. 'Anyway Ace, sit down. We've got business to discuss.'

Ace arranged himself in one of the easy chairs and crossed one well-tailored leg over the other.

'Fire away,' he said.

Joey walked backwards and forwards across the room as he gave a brief account of his meeting with Morton. From time to time Ace nodded approvingly. At the end of the recital Joey seated himself opposite his friend. Ace was very direct.

'What can I do to help?' he enquired.

'I'm getting a team together. Got most of the jobs pencilled in. What I'm short of is a good electronics man, a video expert. He'll be a key part of the operation. Any ideas?'

'Joey, my friend, your troubles are over. You know the Weasel?'

Joey clapped a hand to his forehead.

'Christ. Of course. Just the man. Why didn't I think of him?'

'We often miss the things that are right under our noses,' said Ace sententiously.

'Fix up a meet, will you. Say tomorrow night?'

'Private?' said Ace.

'Very, very private,' said Joey.

'Will do,' said Ace. 'Give you a bell later on today.'

The next day Joey decided to take the first step in his investigation personally. The answers to many of his questions were to be found in any one of the numerous retail shops catering to the public demand for home videos. He chose a large emporium in the West End and entered the premises in the late evening when the homeward-bound commuter would be there in force, having a browse through the titles before catching the train for his home in suburbia. As he expected, the place was crowded.

Joey moved along the shelves where cassettes were ranged in alphabetical order. Every taste was represented in the bewildering array of titles, from downright pornography to classics of the modern cinema. Taking down from the shelves a random selection, giving them a cursory inspection, replacing them and then moving on, Joey glanced from time to time in the direction of the sales counter where three assistants worked at high speed wrapping purchases and taking money. This place is a bloody gold-mine, Joey said to himself.

He noticed that one of the assistants seemed to attract more custom than his colleagues and was on the point of a direct approach when a particularly lurid cover caught his eye. Against a demoniac background of rioting colour appeared the one word 'SNUFF'. Over the title the video was described as 'The original legendary atrocity shot and banned in New York'. A further item of information was that 'The actors and actresses who dedicated their lives to making this film were never seen or heard of again'.

Joey remembered vividly having seen this film once at a private party, behind locked doors. He also recalled the bloody scene in which one of the female participants was mutilated with wire-cutters and an electric saw. Though no stranger to carnage, Joey had been nauseated by the explicit floggings, rapes and castrations which were shown in gory detail. The cassette in his hand, Joey went up to the sales counter and motioned to the salesman whom he had marked out as deserving special attention. He handed over the cassette.

'Thought this one had been banned,' he said.

'Not so far as we know,' said the salesman.

'I'll take it,' said Joey.

'Thank you, sir. Anything else?'

'Any recent releases?'

'The latest we have is Friday Happening.'

Joey recognised the title at once. This was one of Inter-video's copyrights, due for release in a fortnight.

'I'll take it,' he said.

The salesman disappeared through a door into the rear of the shop, shortly emerging with a neatly-wrapped parcel which he placed on the counter.

'That'll be seventy-five pounds, sir,' he said.

Joey paid for the purchase from a thick wad of notes.

'Thank you, sir,' said the salesman. 'Call again.'

Outside the shop Joey hailed a taxi which delivered him to the house in Park Lane. Adgie was adding an unnecessary shine to his pride and joy on the forecourt.

'All right, Adgie,' said Joey.

'All right, sir,' came the brisk reply.

'Hang about. Might need you later.'

'Yessir.'

Inside the house Harry was on duty. He handed Joey a sheaf of messages.

'No problems?' said Joey.

'No problems. Fred and John are on call. Just in case.'

'Right. I'll be upstairs.'

He mounted the stairs to the first floor, where his first task was to open the envelopes containing the messages which had been taken during his absence. The plaintive call from Sir Frederick Morton asking for information on progress was put to one side as deserving of little consideration. For the rest, he noted that Ace had arranged a meeting for ten-thirty that evening at the restaurant, when Weasel would be present. The only other matter of importance was a report from one of his surveillance team. This was a direct lead. Keeping watch on a video shop in North London, the watcher had seen an unmarked delivery van which he described in his own words as being 'a bit iffy'. His suspicions had been confirmed when he caught a glimpse of the driver, a small-time villain from the Peckham manor.

'Followed van,' the report went on. 'Deliveries made at four video shops. Locations attached. Continued following to home base. Warehouse St Katharine's Way, Wapping. Photos of van, driver and premises herewith.'

The watcher was one of four specially selected men equipped with walkie-talkies. Their call-signs were Alpha one, two, three and four respectively. The watcher who had put in the report was Alpha two, the best of the four. Joey recognised the photograph of the van driver, Nicky Nicholls, thick as two short planks, who could be relied on to carry out an order to the letter providing it was given in words of one syllable. Joey picked up the internal phone.

'Harry? Put out a call to Alpha two. Instruction. Continue surveillance and report. Oh, add the words "well done".'

Joey turned his attention to the two videos which he had bought that evening. Removing 'SNUFF' from its box, he slotted the cassette into the player of the television set and settled down to watch the horrifying performance. Suddenly there came the shot he remembered, a close-up of the contorted face of a girl, teeth clenched over a bitten lower lip, blood flowing down her chin and an expression of utter terror in her eyes. In a moment of startling clarity, as he froze the frame, he saw again the unmistakable resemblance to that other face which he had seen on the Gill tapes. He was now sure that they were one and the same.

He switched off the tape and began to pace the room. This was something else. He hadn't just stumbled across a bunch of upper-class sexual perverts playing nasty games in which murder might have a part. Here was an international link which spoke of powerful forces at work behind the scenes, of murders openly committed before the public eye of the television camera. No wonder they wanted me out of the way, thought Joey. I'll have to watch my step.

He ran a part of the other film which had yet to be released by Intervideo and after a few minutes concluded that this was no back-street job carried out by amateurs, but a skilful copying operation done by experts using first-class equipment. Setting up such an operation was a mammoth task involving a huge capital outlay. Throwing a spanner into the works would render the sport of spanner-throwing a very unpopular game in which the players stood a fair chance of meeting a sticky end. Still, thought Joey, in the words of a well-known quizmaster, I've started so I'll finish. There was still a long way to go before the game was played out.

He glanced at his watch, then picked up the internal phone.

'Harry? Tell Adgie I'll be down in ten minutes. Tell him it's Islington.'

Ace Johnson was a womaniser. Despite being married to a woman who, to use his own words, 'takes my breath away every time I look at her', and though Belle was a marvellous mother to his two boys, Ace craved the kind of sexual excitement which could only be provided by what he referred to as 'right little ravers'. His extra-marital activities were something apart from his normal family life, and the small private room at the rear of his restaurant was often the scene of exotic parties for two, where Ace was able to let his trousers down and give free reign to his libido.

On this particular evening the room was not given over to what the proprietor sometimes laughingly referred to as his 'fucking perks'. It was business only. Joey was asking the questions and the Weasel was providing the answers. Ace sat in on the conference as an interested party.

Joey, as usual, had come directly to the point.

'What's the SP on these video pirates?' he said.

The Weasel, ferret-faced, small, wiry and expensively dressed, waved a hand heavily weighted with chunky jewellery.

'Big business,' he said. 'Lot of money being made. Very simple operation. Get hold of a new film. Transfer it to video. Run off thousands of copies. Sell for cash to the retail trade. Bingo. It's a jackpot.'

'How much to set it up?' asked Joey.

'About a hundred grand. Cine two video machine for generating the master. As many duplication machines as you can afford. Going into the business, Joey?'

'Let's say I have an interest in it,' Joey replied. 'Do you know who the top jollies are?'

'No secret,' said the Weasel. 'The Delaney brothers. South London firm. Got a big set-up down by the Tower.'

'Warehouse in St Katharine's Way?'

'That's right. You know all about it then?'

'Not as much as I'd like to know,' said Joey. 'I want a man inside. You're just the ticket.'

'Should be no problem. There's jobs on offer to the right people. What's the proposition?'

'You go in there, find out what's going on, let me know. There's a good drink in it for you.'

'Leave it out, Joey. I'll do it. Never mind about the wages. Things turn out right, give me what you think it's worth. OK?'

'You're on. When do you reckon you can get in?'

'Tomorrow. First thing. Give you a bell around noon.'

'Great. I'll be waiting.'

'OK then. Anything else?'

'I think that's about the lot – for the time being, anyway,' said Joey.

'I'll be off then. See you.'

The little man rose to his feet and Ace accompanied him to the door. Returning to his seat, Ace poured a liberal measure of his favourite Armagnac.

'What's the form then, Joey?' he enquired.

'I'll know better tomorrow. After I've heard from the Weasel. Can you come over to Park Lane tomorrow? Say about half-twelve?'

'Sure. Is it action stations?'

'May well be,' said Joey.

It was shortly after eleven in the morning and Joey and the Duchess were in the closing stages of a strenuous work-out.

'Coming along nicely,' he said. 'How d'you feel with the knuckle-dusters? Getting used to them?'

Francesca regarded the palms of her hands, where dull bruises were beginning to show. She shook her head ruefully.

'I'll be glad when I can start hurting somebody. That heavy bag doesn't squeal.'

Joey laughed. 'You've knocked the stuffing out of it at any rate,' he said. 'Have to get a new one in. Remind me to tell Harry.'

'One more bash,' she said. The near-naked body flashed across the floor. Pivoting on the ball of her left foot she shot a brass-knuckled fist at the bag. The main seam gave way and the stuffing spilled out. She gave a delighted yell.

'Well done, Duchess,' said Joey. 'Dead as a doornail. Turn out the burial party.'

Showered and dressed, they were drinking coffee when the call from the Weasel came through.

'Go ahead. The call's being taped,' said Joey.

'Right,' said the voice. 'Got the job, started already. It's a straight operation. Private limited company. Everything on the books except the skim off the top. Manager chap called Bernie Harrison. Married, two kids. Lives out at Hounslow. Drives Renault five saloon, blue, C registration. He's bent. Two other geezers on the technical side. Three heavies from the Delaney mob. That's the lot. Be in touch later.'

The line went dead. Joey replaced the receiver and immediately got on to Marion on the internal phone.

'Get this tape transcribed. Dig out what you can on one Bernie Harrison of Hounslow. List the details. Put out a call to Alphas one to four. Target warehouse, St Katharine's Way, maintain surveillance, hourly reports, log them. All clear?'

'All clear, Mr Bello.'

Joey replaced the handset and turned to Francesca.

'It's on, Duchess,' he said. 'Action stations. Ace will be along shortly. We have a job to do, just the three of us. Ready?'

The light of battle was in Francesca's eye.

'Aye aye, mon général,' she said. 'Ready, willing and able.'

Mister Bernard Harrison of 12 Acacia Close in the borough of Hounslow was well pleased with life. He spread chunky marmalade on a slice of hot buttered toast and regarded his wife fondly across the breakfast table. The boys had already departed for school. They were alone in the detached house which, though not luxurious, was eminently comfortable.

He finished off the remains of his coffee, wiped his lips with a crisp napkin and rose to his feet.

'See you later, darling. Usual time,' he said. He went round the table and kissed her on the forehead.

'Very well, dear,' said his wife.

The morning was clear and bright. Overhead a plane on its descent to Heathrow traced a white vapour trail against the blue sky. Harrison, a careful man, edged the blue Renault out of the drive and looked both ways before emerging onto the main road. He saw nothing suspicious about the black Mercedes which followed at a discreet distance and was taken by surprise when, with a blast of its powerful horn, the Mercedes drew alongside and the blonde in the passenger seat waved him into the side of the road.

As the Mercedes braked to a halt a few yards ahead, the blonde alighted and walked rapidly towards him. What followed was like a bad dream. The blonde yanked open the driver's side door and put a hand casually on the nape of his neck. A sudden surge of pain mounted to the top of his head and, through the singing in his ears, he heard a voice telling him to move over. Automatically he straddled the gear lever and almost fell into the passenger seat.

The Renault moved off and fell into position behind the black Mercedes. The two cars threaded their way through a succession of narrow lanes. From time to time the girl at the wheel of the Renault stretched out a hand and pressed with finger and thumb on the neck of the semi-conscious man beside her.

The end of Harrison's nightmare journey came when the Mercedes nosed its way into the yard adjacent to a small cottage in the middle of nowhere. Harrison heard himself feebly protesting as he was helped from his seat and led into the cottage by two men, one of them black, the other white. Still in a daze, he found himself sitting in a chair. He regained full consciousness as the blonde held a glass of water to his lips.

'Is he all right now, Duchess?' said the white man.

'Right as rain, Joey,' said the girl.

Harrison licked his lips and tried to speak but was only able to manage a strangled moan.

'Now, Mr Harrison,' said the man addressed as Joey. 'I'm going to ask you some questions. Just be a good boy and answer them and you'll be all right.'

Harrison looked at his questioner. He saw a pair of piercing eyes set in a tanned face down which ran a livid scar. It was the face of a man who meant what he said.

'You're Bernie Harrison,' said Joey. 'You are running a pirate video operation for the Delaney brothers. Right?'

'I . . . I . . . don't know what . . .'

Joey stepped forward. Quite deliberately he struck Harrison a heavy blow in the face.

'Right?' he repeated.

'Yes . . . Yes. Don't hit me . . .'

The remorseless voice continued. 'You're in full charge of things at St Katharine's Way?'

This time the response was instantaneous. 'Yes.'

'Good. Now listen carefully. My colleagues here are experts in inflicting pain.' He gestured toward Francesca and Ace. Ace toyed with a wicked-looking knife. Francesca bared her teeth in a savage grin. Harrison's heart sank. Tears came to his eyes.

'You are going to do exactly what I tell you,' Joey went on. 'First, who's in charge if you're absent?'

'Jimmy . . . Jimmy Foster.'

'Right. You're going to speak to him on the phone. You'll tell him that you're doing a bit of work at home. The wife isn't feeling well. You'll tell him to send over some documents you need. They are cash customers' files, bank paying-in book, staff records, work in progress and the private ledger. Got it?'

Harrison was terror-stricken as he regarded the three implacable faces confronting him. He felt the wet warmth between his legs as he lost control of his bladder.

'Yes . . . yes . . . I understand.'

'Tell Foster to send the stuff over with that chap you took on yesterday. Remember?'

'Yes. The Weasel. Franklyn Arbuthnot.'

Joey and Ace exchanged glances. Bloody Nora, thought Joey, what a name to be born with.

'You're doing fine,' said Joey. 'Now pull yourself together. When you speak to Foster not one slip-up, not a single mistake, or it will cost me a lot of money and you'll be a dead man.'

The telephone was on a small table at Harrison's elbow. Joey consulted a scrap of paper and dialled a number. As a click announced that the connection had been made, he handed the receiver to Harrison.

For a man in a complete state of terror, Harrison behaved very credibly, repeating Joey's instructions to the letter. As he put down the receiver Joey patted him on the head.

'There now,' he said. 'Wasn't very painful, was it?'

Harrison's eyes closed as he fell off the chair in a dead faint.

'We'll be off now, Duchess,' said Joey. 'Keep our friend here for an hour, then drive him to Heathrow. Point him in the direction of home, give him a pat on the head and tell him to keep his mouth shut. Collect your own car from the park. See you back at the office.'

At three-thirty that afternoon Joey and Francesca attended on Sir Frederick by appointment at the latter's office. Without preamble Joey placed a bulky package on Morton's desk, on top of which he laid a single sheet of notepaper.

'There's my report. Private and confidential. Not to be disclosed to any third party. The package contains all the evidence you will need to carry out a successful prosecution against the biggest pirating operation in the country. They were handed to me voluntarily by an ex-employee.'

'Excellent, excellent.' Sir Frederick rubbed his hands together. 'I'll get my security chief on to it at once. Can I offer you some tea . . .'

'Thanks, no. We're rather busy, so we'll get along,' said Joey. Ignoring Morton's outstretched hand he turned to Francesca.

'Come along, Duchess,' he said.

Three hours had elapsed since his visit to Morton's office. Joey was going through a sheaf of reports when the call from the Chairman of Intervideo came through. He had been expecting it. The man was clearly in a rage.

'Bello,' he shouted, 'what the hell are you playing at. The police have just raided this warehouse place. Empty. Bare as a bone . . .'

'Are you in your office?' asked Joey.

'Of course. Where else . . .'

'I'll be with you in fifteen minutes,' said Joey.

Sir Frederick was still seething when Joey arrived. Spluttering with rage, the little man launched into the attack.

'Look here, Bello,' he shouted. 'Don't play games with me . . .'

'Shut up, sit down and listen,' said Joey. 'If you hadn't called me, I was just about to call you. What did you do with the dossier I gave you?'

'Handed it over to my chief of security. I instructed him to take it to the police immediately.'

Joey extracted some papers from his pocket.

'I've had this warehouse under surveillance all day. These are the reports. At four o'clock a removal van turned up and cleared the place. The equipment they removed is now in premises at Shadwell. Here is the address. The police raided the warehouse at *six*. What do you make of that?'

'Well, my security man had to get down to Scotland Yard . . .'

'Which took him all of two hours? Rubbish. Your security man tipped off Delaney's mob, wandered down to Scotland Yard via the Blackwall Tunnel and that's the size of it. I did the job this way so that your man would incriminate himself. My advice to you is to get into a taxi, go and see one of your high-up pals at the Yard and tell him the whole story. You can sack your chief of security tomorrow, that is if the law doesn't get him before then.'

Sir Frederick was suitably deflated. He sank back in his chair.

'What can I say . . .' he began.

'Nothing,' said Joey. 'Just pay my bill when it falls due. Goodnight.'

5. Politics is a Dirty Game

To a man who has spent several years of his life locked up within the grim walls of a prison, freedom is a precious commodity. No less precious are the sight and smell of green grass, the leaves of a tree rustling in a summer breeze and the feeling of being surrounded by people scurrying to and fro, which is part of the magic of a large city.

From the windows of his private domain, Joey had all of these things in the vast expanse of Hyde Park rolling westward into the infinite distance, in the constant flow of humanity crowding the pavements of Park Lane and the knowledge that he was now a part of the action and not a detached observer.

His musings were interrupted as Francesca entered the room. She had come straight from the gym, her face devoid of make-up, her hair combed back and held by a clip in the nape of her neck.

'Morning, Duchess,' said Joey.

'Morning, Joey. I've ordered coffee. It's on the way up. What's the news?'

Joey adopted the plummy voice of a BBC newsreader.

'The Government is facing a minor revolt . . .'

'Nark it, Joey. The Government is always facing a revolt. They're a revolting lot anyway.'

'Say that again.' As he uttered the words, Jane entered with the coffee tray.

'Thanks, Jane,' said Joey. 'Put it on the table.' As Jane left the room he moved to the window and stood for a few moments deep in thought. He turned to his companion.

'Sit down,' he said. 'I want to talk to you.'

'I'm listening,' she said. She sat back in an easy chair, tucking her feet under her. Joey sat in a facing seat.

'It's now almost the end of July. We've pulled off a couple

of jobs, made quite a nice bit of money,' Joey began. 'How do you feel about things now?'

'Just the same as I did before. I'm in and I want to stay in.'

'Sure?'

'Bloody certain.'

'You know, I'm a bit older than you,' said Joey. 'I've met women who've wanted to go it alone, compete in a man's world on equal terms with men. There was Beryl Gibbons. She ran the Thomas à Beckett pub in the Old Kent Road. The fellow she lived with, Tommy Gibbons, was a bloody good fighter and a very respected man. When he died Beryl took over the pub. She was a remarkable woman. Unfortunately she's now passed away too.'

'I've heard about her,' said Francesca.

'At one time she was the only woman boxing promoter in the world. All the big names, Muhammad Ali, Henry Cooper, Sugar Ray Leonard – you name them, she knew them. There was a fully-equipped gym over the pub. All the champions used it for sparring sessions, John Conteh, Alan Minter, Terry Downes and a lot of others.'

'What happened to her?'

'Oh, she got turfed out of the pub. It's a sad story. She was there for more than twenty years, she owed a few grand so she collected the shitty end of the stick. That was her lot.'

'Sounds like a really tough lady,' said Francesca.

'It knocked her sideways. Still, she had a good giggle before she left.'

'Tell me.'

'Well, she organised a big charity send off for the Commonwealth boxing team. Invited a lot of faces. Heard of Cynthia Payne?'

'The madam from Streatham. Of course. They made that film about her.'

'That's the one. Madame Sin, the luncheon voucher queen. She turned up with a right bevy of beauties, half-a-dozen or so. The press photographers were there, so what does one of the birds do but pop her boobs out right in front of them.

Dunno if it affected the lads in the team, but they missed out on the gold medals when they went to Brisbane to compete in the Commonwealth Games! Three of them got silver but the other four got nowhere.' Joey laughed.

'I suppose that proves something,' said Francesca. 'What was she like, this Madame Sin?'

'Bloody marvellous. She'd just done six months for keeping a brothel, but she was laughing and joking, the life of the party. And the birds she brought with her . . . They were smashers.'

'How many of them did you screw?'

Joey laughed again. 'A gentleman never tells,' he grinned.

'No?' she replied. 'You've just told me.'

'Well, keep it to yourself,' said Joey. 'Let's change the subject. We've a bit of business to discuss.'

'Go ahead.'

'Does the name Sir Charles Macowan mean anything to you?'

'Oh, yes. An MP. I went to a party once at his flat in Cadogan Square. He's very rich. What about him?'

'Had a call from him this morning. Said I'd been recommended by a friend. He reckons his wife has gone off the rails. Wants me to get evidence for a divorce. I told him it wasn't our line of country. Anyway, he persuaded me to have a meet. I'm going to see him this evening. What do you think?'

'Wonder who gave him your name?'

'He didn't say.'

Francesca pondered for a moment. 'I agree it's not up our street. Still, it might open up a few doors. I'd go and see him. Want me to come along?'

'Don't think so,' said Joey. 'I'll see what the form is. We can talk about it later.'

'Good. By the way, apropos our little talk about women in a man's world. I don't see myself ending up in a pub, but I do rather fancy running a brothel. How does that grab you?'

‘Piss off,’ said Joey.

Cadogan Square in the heartland of Belgravia is high on the list of London’s desirable residences. Joey was admitted to Sir Charles Macowan’s house by an impeccably garbed butler.

‘Sir Charles is expecting you, sir,’ he said. ‘Would you come this way.’

Joey followed the man through a richly-carpeted hallway and into a wide passage that led to the rear of the house. Here the butler paused and knocked softly on an imposing oak door.

‘Come in,’ said a voice from inside the room.

The butler opened the door and ushered Joey into the presence of the master of the house.

The room, obviously a study, was a masterpiece of sophisticated elegance. Deep carpet, panelled walls, glass-fronted bookcases and furniture that would not have looked out of place in the Victoria and Albert museum, added up to an atmosphere of quiet opulence that was complemented by the aroma of Havana tobacco. The man who came forward to meet Joey was of a piece with the background. Tall and good-looking, in his middle forties, a patrician face surmounted by carefully groomed hair silver-streaked at the temples, he was the image of the successful politician. He shook Joey’s hand. His grip was warm and firm.

‘Mr Bello. I’m so pleased to meet you. It was very kind of you to come.’

His voice was a politician’s voice, deep and mellow and completely insincere.

‘Good evening, Sir Charles. Glad to make your acquaintance,’ said Joey.

‘Sit down, my dear fellow, sit down. What would you like to drink?’

‘A little Scotch with a lot of soda,’ said Joey.

His host busied himself at a small table in the corner of the room, returning with two glasses which he placed on an occasional table within reach of Joey's hand. Drawing up a chair, he sat down opposite his guest.

'Well,' he began, 'I've heard so much about you I feel I know you already.'

'From whom?' said Joey.

'Oh, no secret. Freddie Morton. He told me that you had rendered him a considerable service . . .'

'Did he specify what it was?'

'Good Lord, no. Soul of discretion, our Freddie. Merely said that if I wanted a tip-top man for some – ah – discreet enquiries, I should get in touch with you.'

Bloody liar, thought Joey. Morton had in all probability described him as an ex-villain with a lot of low cunning who would go to any lengths to get results. Joey decided to play the game according to the rules.

'That was very good of him, Sir Charles . . .'

'Come now, let's drop the formalities. Charlie to you. It's Joey isn't it?'

The bugger knows more about me than he's letting on, thought Joey.

'That's right,' he said.

'Well, Joey, we politicians must watch our step. We're very vulnerable to scandal . . .'

'Yes. I have noticed it,' said Joey drily.

Macowan roared with laughter. 'I say, I like that. Very good. But don't run away with the idea that I've put some starlet in the pudding club. It's nothing like that.'

'So what is it then?'

'It's a very delicate matter indeed. It concerns my wife. I have every reason to think that she's – er – not behaving herself.'

'Really. In what way?'

'Well, she's been seen around. Night clubs, drunken parties and that sort of thing. Mixing with some questionable characters. You know what I mean, Joey.'

'Yes, Charlie. What you're saying is that she's been dropping her knickers for anybody with a stiff prick and no conscience.'

Macowan cleared his throat. 'Er – couldn't have put it better myself. I say, old chap, you have – er – a very nice turn of phrase. Now drink up and let me get you the other half.'

Joey swallowed the remainder of his Scotch. It was very strong. So that's his game, he thought, trying to get me pissed, a little test to see how discreet I can be.

Macowan brought the replenished glasses to the table. As he sat down he gave Joey the full benefit of his expensively-dentured politician's smile.

'Freddie Morton gave you quite a build-up,' he said. 'What did you do for him? In strict confidence between us, of course.'

'Charlie, I'm surprised at you,' Joey replied. 'You should know better than to ask such a question. Dealings between myself and a client are strictly confidential.'

Macowan nodded and picked up his glass. 'Bottoms up,' he said, gulping the contents. Joey followed suit.

'I feel like a drop of the old bubbly,' said Macowan. 'How about splitting a bottle with me?'

'Good idea,' said Joey. 'Wheel it in.'

'I've got some of the widow on ice. Veuve Clicquot, y'know.'

'Couldn't be better.' Joey laughed inwardly. He had in his time drunk bigger and better boozers than Macowan under the table. He knew he would have to sweat the alcohol out of his system the following morning, but that was another day.

The champagne on the table between them and two glasses poured, Macowan re-opened the conversation.

'I like the way you go about things, Joey,' he said. 'You're very straightforward. No beating about the bush. Hope you don't mind my saying this but I looked up your pedigree. Been through quite a bit in your time, haven't you?'

'I've been a villain,' said Joey. 'Now I'm going straight, all debts paid and a clean sheet. I've served a hard apprenticeship, now I'm cashing in.'

'Jolly good luck to you. Drink up.'

Joey did as he was bidden. His host lost no time in re-filling the glasses.

'Now let's get down to business,' said Joey. 'First of all, as I told you, I'm not in the divorce racket. I run an expensive operation and my fees are high . . .'

'I'm not bothered about what it will cost,' said Macowan. 'I want the best and I'm willing to pay for it.'

'Right, we're agreed on that. Now, what exactly do you want?'

'A comprehensive report on her. Where she goes, what she does, who's screwing her and where and when. Everything watertight so she can't wriggle out of it.'

'That's very clear,' said Joey.

'I'll give you a retainer now. What do you suggest?'

'Five thousand on account. Balance payable on completion of job and acceptance of report. Agreed?'

'It's a deal.' Macowan took out his cheque book, made out the cheque and handed it to Joey, who put it in his pocket without even glancing at it.

'Good. That's settled,' said Macowan. 'Now let's have another drink.'

Two bottles of Veuve Clicquot later, Joey took his leave. Macowan escorted him to the door, where he shook hands vigorously.

'It's been a pleasure to meet you, Joey,' he said. 'I'll see you again soon?'

'You will,' said Joey. 'I'll be in touch.'

The following morning Joey was up bright and early. In the park he did a couple of miles of road work, sweating the champagne out of his system. Back in the gym he donned light leather gloves and handed out severe punishment to the heavy bag for some ten minutes, following up with a session on the parallel bars and ending with fifty press-ups. Emerging from the shower, he literally bumped into Francesca.

'Morning, Duchess,' he said. 'You've saved me a phone call.'

'Credit it to my expense account,' she said. 'Did you take on the Macowan job?'

'Yes. I've called Ace in. He'll be here in half an hour. Join us upstairs?'

'Will do,' she said.

By the time Ace and Francesca had joined him, Joey had taped a precis of his meeting with Macowan. As they took their seats round the table, he gave them a brief run-down on the proceedings of the previous evening.

'Very forthcoming character, our Charlie,' he said. 'We had a good drink. What he wants is a dossier on his wife's little games. I've taken the job. He paid five grand up front.'

'So we take him to the cleaners,' said Francesca.

'That's about the size of it,' said Joey. 'Marion's getting a profile on the bloke. What do you know, Duchess?'

'Quite a lot,' she said.

'Put it on tape,' said Joey. He handed her the miniature recorder. Francesca pressed the button and began to speak.

'Lady Lydia Macowan. Maiden name Wentworth. Married to Sir Charles Macowan, back bench Conservative MP, for ten years. No children. Had numerous affairs, one night stands and some rough trade. List of names can be provided. Does a lot of charity work. Committee member, Ladies' Society of Christian Purity. Said to be mistress of the treasurer, Lord Smythe . . .'

'OK, that's enough for the moment,' said Joey. 'Gives us something to work on.'

'Where do I fit in?' asked Ace.

'I thought we'd handle it together,' said Joey. 'Not a big job. Follow her around, get a few compromising pictures, have a bit of a giggle and get paid for it.'

'Right. When do we begin?' asked Ace.

'I'll start the ball rolling,' said Joey. 'Tomorrow morning I'll follow her around, just get the feel of things. After that we play it by ear.'

Lady Lydia Macowan left the marital home at ten-thirty in the morning. At precisely eleven o'clock she was lying on her back on the floor of a flat in Sloane Avenue, the subject of a vigorous screwing by a short fat man who, to judge by his rapturous cries, was enjoying the experience immensely. The woman lay like a log, responding not at all to the thrusting of her partner. When finally, reacting to a particularly violent lunge, she stirred and gave an indication that she was about to take an active part in the proceedings, the man ground himself into her, using every ounce of his weight to pin her to the carpet.

'Lie still, you cow, lie still,' he hissed. 'I've told you before. Just lie still.'

Tears of frustration welled in her eyes as she controlled her natural instincts and, as the lunging continued, she bit hard on her lower lip. Finally the man climaxed and collapsed on top of her, a dead weight. After a while he disengaged himself and rolled over on his back, his flaccid penis hanging forlornly between his legs.

'Go on. You know what to do,' he said. 'Clean it.'

This was the part she hated most. Leaning over his parted legs, the smell of semen in her nostrils, she put out her tongue and began to lick. The man leaned back and closed his eyes, a look of beatific contentment on his face. After what seemed hours to the woman, he opened his eyes.

'Get dressed and go,' he said. 'Don't be late tomorrow.'

Whilst this bizarre performance had been going on, Joey was engaged in conversation with the porter of the block, who had at first been reluctant to give out any information until Joey had waved a fifty pound note under his nose. The smell of money unlocked his tongue.

'Oh, yes,' he said. 'She comes here every morning. Visits Lord Smythe. Stays for about half an hour. When she comes out she looks as though she's been well shagged. Not a bad-looking tart either. Too good for that bald-headed little bastard.'

Joey said 'thanks' and left the foyer. From the opposite side of the road he watched the woman as she descended the steps to street level. She did indeed give every appearance of having been well shagged and, from the despondent slump of her shoulders, also gave the impression that she had not enjoyed it.

As she walked in the direction of King's Road, Joey followed her. When she turned into the main thoroughfare her shoulders straightened and her step became brisker. A few yards along the road was a small pub which she entered without hesitation. Joey was close on her heels, brushing past her and going towards the end of the bar from where he would have a good view of what happened.

She was obviously no stranger to this watering hole in the King's Road. The group of three young men standing at the bar had looked towards the door as she entered, and one of them broke away and went forward to meet her. Sloane Ranger was written all over him.

'Lydia, my darling, you look ravishing,' he said. His voice reached every corner of the bar. 'Let me get you a little dwinkie-poo. What is it? The usual?'

She nodded and the young man turned to the barman.

'Leslie, a large gin and tonic for her ladyship.'

Lydia's metamorphosis from dejected middle age to youthful life and soul of the party was immediate and startling. She gave the three young men the benefit of a brilliant smile, embraced each one in turn and perched herself on a stool which one of her admirers had obligingly placed behind her. Joey ordered a light ale and, one elbow on the bar counter, settled back to watch the comedy.

That she was on intimate terms with her three companions was in no doubt. As she took a hefty swig of her drink, she crossed her legs, displaying a considerable length of shapely thigh as she did so.

'Don't show us your knickers yet, darling,' said the young man who had first welcomed her.

'Derek darling, you know I never wear them,' she said gaily. She turned to the others.

'How are you, Tony? Freddie? Haven't seen you for yonks.'

'Ready, willing and able,' said Tony. He grinned at his friends, a grin that said quite plainly, come on, lads, let's get her tanked up and then have her away for an afternoon session.

Joey moved back further into his corner, took out his pocket telephone and tapped out the office number. The connection made, he spoke softly.

'Ace there?' he said. He waited a few moments. 'Ace. I'm in a pub. King's Road, Chelsea. Opposite Smith Street. Get here, pronto.'

During the time that elapsed before Ace made an appearance, some fifteen minutes or so, Lady Lydia had downed six gin and tonics. The three men were clustered round her, standing very close. Though he could not see what was going on, Joey was sure that Lydia was caressing their private parts under cover of the bar counter. Blimey, what a raver, he was thinking, when Ace came through the door and made his way to the corner where Joey sat.

'Hi, Ace,' Joey said. 'What'll you drink?'

Ace pulled up a stool and seated himself. 'Just a beer,' he said. He made an almost imperceptible gesture. 'That the lady?'

'That's the lady,' said Joey.

'He doesn't keep her short,' said Ace. 'That's a Dior suit she's wearing. Looks a bit rumpled.'

'Yeah. She's been at it this morning. I've got to make a few enquiries about a member of the Upper House . . .'

'Up 'er what?' said Ace.

'That's right. Up 'er arse,' said Joey. 'Now you take over from here. From what I can see there's a foursome coming off, so keep an eye on where they go. We'll have a meet later on and you can put me in the picture. See you later.'

Joey made his way to the door. As he passed the carousing group he gave them a casual glance. He had been correct in his surmise that some under the counter work was going on. Masked by the surrounding bodies but just visible from his angle, Tony's penis was being gently massaged by the ardent fingers of Lady Lydia.

★

Francesca and Joey were going over a profile of Lord Smythe when Ace arrived to put in his report of the afternoon's doings. He was in high spirits.

'I think the case is pretty well wrapped up, my friends,' he said.

'You don't say,' said Joey. 'What happened?'

'Well,' Ace began, 'just after you left, her ladyship spotted me and wandered over. Started to chat me up. Her friends didn't like that very much so they came over and tried to get her away. They were all nicely pissed, so no problem, I gave them the old smooge and we were soon palsy walsy. They invite me to this party they're going to have. We pile into a taxi and end up in a classy pad in Eaton Square. No sooner do we get inside than her ladyship whips off her skirt. She's stark bollock naked under it. Now, she says, I'm going to have a gourmet meal. I'll have Tony for starter, because he's long and thin and appetising. Then for the main dish I'll have Derek. He's more than a mouthful. Freddie for dessert. He's sweet. Then she gives me a look and says she'll finish off with a large black for coffee.'

Joey and Francesca were laughing their heads off.

'You say she was pissed,' said Joey.

'Very,' said Ace.

'Wonderful what it does for the imagination. Carry on.'

'Well, she slobbered her bibful. She falls back on a big settee with her legs waving in the air. Tony was in like a flash, rams it into her. The other two queue up with their pricks in their hands. Yours truly is in the background. Lucky I have the Candid Camera with me.'

He took out the small camera, no larger than a cigarette lighter, and laid it on the table.

'You got the lot?' said Joey.

'Thirty-five frames of it. Tony shoots his load, then staggers off. Derek and Freddie have a bash. Comes to my turn her ladyship has passed out.'

'So what did you do?' queried Francesca.

'I did a gutter press reporter.'

'What's that?'

'Well, Duchess, I made my excuses and left.'

'You've done a fine job, Ace. That the lot?' said Joey.

'That's it. Oh, before I forget. Care to come to a party?'

'Where and when?'

'The Quagmire Club. Tonight. It'll be high society camp. Some well-known faces will be there.'

'Might be useful,' said Joey. 'What about you, Duchess? Care to come along?'

'No dice. Strictly male,' said Ace.

'So that lets me out. Well, you two go along and tell me all about it in the morning.'

Sheriton Crescent in the heart of Belgravia is a quiet backwater whose serenity is rarely disturbed by anything more important than a slight altercation between residents as to who should park where and when. The discreetly curtained windows give little hint of what goes on in the elegant Victorian drawing rooms and bedrooms.

From the outside, number 69 was no exception to the rule. Only a closed circle were privy to the activities of the all-male members of the Quagmire Club, which had been established in those pre-Wolfenden days when sexual relations between consenting adults came within the purview of the criminal law. Now, in the more relaxed and tolerant atmosphere towards those who practised 'the love that dare not speak its name', membership of the club was confined to the rich and famous.

The taxi deposited Joey and Ace outside number 69 as Big Ben chimed eleven. Ace pressed the bell-push, there was a delay of a few seconds and the door opened. The two men passed into a spacious entrance hall to be confronted by a slim young man whose self-possessed air and quiet manner gave no indication of his skill in the martial arts. Here's a guy who's a killer, thought Joey as he looked into the pale blue eyes.

'Mr Johnson,' said the young man. 'Mr Benson is expecting you. Go straight through, please.'

He opened a secondary door and stood aside as Ace and Joey passed into an enormous room where some fifty men in various stages of undress were giving free rein to their sexual imaginings. The scene almost beggared description. Bent double on a settee, a young man, naked save for riding boots and spurs, demonstrated the ultimate in self-gratification as he mouthed the end of his own twelve-inch erection. The small crowd surrounding him burst into spontaneous applause as he ejaculated and swallowed the end-product of his endeavours. In other parts of the luxuriously-furnished room every known form of sexual depravity was on display, buggery and fellatio being the most general.

'Blimey,' said Joey, 'it's unbelievable.'

They were pounced upon by a small man, incongruously garbed in a pair of gaudy boxer shorts.

'Ace, my darling,' he cried. 'So nice of you to come. Who's your lovely friend?'

Ace performed the introduction.

'Joey Bello, Benny Benson,' he said.

Benson shook Joey warmly by the hand.

'Come along, come along,' he said. 'You're both called to the bar. Champagne in profusion – or anything else you want.'

The bar was situated in an ante-room. There, preliminary groping seemed to be the order of the day, and Joey recognised many faces familiar to him, faces he had seen on the television screen and in the pages of the popular press. As he drank a glass of excellent champagne, his host tugged at his sleeve.

'Feel free to join in whenever you wish,' he said.

'Thanks very much,' said Joey, but no thanks, he thought to himself.

Ace was draped on a corner of the bar. The entrance of the handsome West Indian had not gone unnoticed. A beautiful youth, dressed in a Roman-style toga, advanced toward him.

'Hello, darling. I fancy a bit of chocolate. How about you?'

'Go suck a Mars bar,' said Ace. 'Can't you see I'm with a friend?'

'Oh, sorry. Perhaps I'll see you later,' said the youth.

'Not if I see you first,' said Ace.

With an indolent wave of his hand the youth departed. Ace turned to Joey with a grin.

'Nearly got caught there,' he said. 'What do you think of the show anyway?'

'What can I say?' Joey replied. 'I thought I'd seen it all.'

'You ain't seen nothing yet,' said Ace.

After midnight, as though at a given signal, the crowd of revellers began to pair off and disappear in the direction of what were obviously private rooms in other parts of the house. Benson, after an abortive attempt to interest Joey and Ace in a gleesome threesome, departed in a huff.

'I've seen all I want to see,' said Joey. 'How about having it away?'

'Suits me,' said Ace.

'I'll just have a slash first,' said Joey. 'Hang about.'

The toilets were on a par with the rest of the house. Approaching the stalls, Joey recognised a familiar back. He took his place in an adjoining compartment.

'Hello, Charlie,' he said.

Sir Charles Macowan turned. 'Why, hello Joey,' he said. 'What are you doing here?'

'Pursuing my enquiries,' said Joey with a mischievous grin. 'What about you?'

'Well, a politician sometimes finds himself in some – ah – queer places.' Macowan peered over the edge of his stall. 'That's a handy old weapon you've got there,' he said.

'Private. Ladies only. Not to be used for shit-stabbing.'

As they washed their hands at adjoining basins, Macowan asked the question.

'Any news for me, Joey?'

'I don't discuss business in pisshouses,' said Joey. 'I have a result for you. I'll give you a bell in the morning. OK?'

'Look forward to hearing from you,' said Macowan.

In the taxi that transported Joey and Ace back to Park Lane, the two men discussed the implications of Macowan's presence at the Quagmire.

'No messing, the guy's as queer as a clockwork orange,' said Ace.

'Anybody who gets an invite to a Benny Benson party has got to have the right credentials. Remember the little fellow on the door?'

'Not half,' said Joey. 'A bloody killer.'

'That's what I mean,' said Ace. 'I'll tell you something else. If the worst comes to the worst, they know how to dispose of bodies.'

All of which gave Joey food for thought when the cab dropped him off at the house in Park Lane.

At eleven o'clock the following morning, Macowan and Joey were closeted in the study of Macowan's house. Joey, after his morning work-out, was at his best, his mind clear and alert. His host, in stark contrast, was suffering after what must have been a night of prolonged debauchery. Despite Macowan's offer of a hair of the dog, Joey elected to drink coffee. Donning the mantle of bluff heartiness, part of the politician's armoury, Macowan came straight to the point.

'Well now, Joey,' he said. 'You told me you had a result. What have you got for me?'

Joey took from his briefcase a bulky manilla envelope and placed it on the table between them.

'Here's my report. It's undeniable evidence, supported by photographs, of your wife's infidelity. If you intend to go for divorce, you won't need anything further.'

Macowan opened the envelope and went through the contents, reading rapidly the attested statements and spending some time on a perusal of the colour photographs.

'You've done a first-class job, Joey,' he said finally. 'Is there anything else I ought to know?'

'So far as I'm concerned I've done my job,' said Joey. 'The rest is up to you.'

'So what's your honest opinion?'

'You really want to hear it?'

'I'd value it. You're a man of the world. So am I.'

'All right. From where I sit, this is the situation,' said Joey. 'I can understand a man loving another man, but buggered – excuse the pun – if I can understand why they should stick their pricks up each other's arses to prove it. Still, that's your way of life and you're entitled to it. So far as your relations with your wife are concerned, it's six of one and half a dozen of the other. She doesn't get it at home so she goes looking for it elsewhere. I'm sorry for both of you.'

Macowan gave a wry smile. 'A typical heterosexual viewpoint,' he said. 'You don't understand, and I don't suppose you ever will. So, as you say, you've done your job. What do I owe you?'

'Nothing. You've paid me a retainer, so let's leave it like that. I didn't want the job in the first place. I'll get along now. Don't bother to see me out.'

The sun shone on Cadogan Square. Above the din of the Sloane Street traffic he heard the chatter of a lawn mower and the smell of new-mown grass came to his nostrils. As he hailed a taxi he somehow had the feeling that he had emerged from a dungheap into the pure, clear light of day.

On the forecourt of the house in Park Lane, Adgie was adding a further lustre to the already spotless Jaguar. As Joey alighted from the taxi, the little man came up to him.

'Can I have a word?' he said.

'Go ahead,' said Joey.

'There's a whisper going round. Somebody's put a contract out on you. Heard anything?'

'I was expecting something. What's the word?'

'A firm from Cable Street. I've got a name. Hippie Palmer. Ring a bell?'

Joey nodded. 'It certainly does. I'll have to make a few enquiries. Thanks, Adgie.'

The little man's face fell. 'Can't I make one?' he said plaintively. 'I'm a bit pissed off, hanging about, polishing the motor.'

'Course you can. I'll be out in a couple of minutes, then we'll drive down the boozer and do a bit of earwigging. OK?'

'Bloody lovely,' said Adgie.

The Warwick Arms in the Portobello Road is a favourite haunt of the hounds from the Dale. At one time it had been run by Ruby Sparks, a notorious jewel thief and one of the few who had managed to make it over the wall from Dartmoor. When Joey walked in, closely followed by Adgie, the present incumbent greeted him warmly.

'Joey. Long time no see,' he said. 'What'll you have?'

'Scotch and coke for me,' said Joey.

'Mine's a split tonic, plenty of ice,' said Adgie.

The landlord bustled away to execute the order. As he did so, Joey looked round the bar. A familiar face caught his eye and he raised a hand in recognition. Freddie Murphy, well-known on the other side of the water, left the small group of men with whom he was drinking and came up to Joey, a wide smile on his face, a hand outstretched.

'Joey, my son,' he said. 'Nice to see you. How're you doing?'

'Mustn't grumble,' said Joey. 'What about you?'

'No complaints, no complaints at all. By the way, seen Eddie and Charlie recently?'

Mention of the Richardson brothers took Joey back to the time when, along with two others, he had escorted Charlie back to Cordingley open prison. The elder Richardson had been granted week-end leave so that, according to officialdom, he would have a chance to accustom himself to life on the outside in preparation for his release on parole. He had left the prison in a Rolls Royce. He was to return less stylishly in a humble Ford Cortina, having been AWOL for twelve hours.

Joey had been present, among a host of family and friends, as Charlie celebrated his short spell of freedom. Present also were the representatives of the press to whom Charlie was news with a capital N. So, when the object of their attentions failed to report at the appointed hour, the hunt was up, with reporters and their attendant photographers combing South London for traces of the fugitive.

It was imperative that Charlie should return to Cordingley under his own steam, for a nicking while on the run would militate against his chances of release on parole. So it was that the anonymous red Cortina, driven by one of Charlie's friends and carrying, in addition to the returning prisoner, Joey and another man, sped along the road to Bisley under cover of darkness.

It was then that the comedy began. Arriving at Cordingley the quartet ran into a press and television reception worthy of minor royalty. The prison was in comparative darkness. Charlie, Joey and their two companions leapt from the car, made for the gates and launched a determined assault on the final barrier between the returning prisoner and his objective. Charlie put his finger on the bell and kept it there while Joey and the other two men bellowed demands for admittance. The photographers crowded in to get a clear shot of their quarry. Joey, holding his hat in front of Charlie's face, pointed his camera at the newsmen and let off flash after flash, effectively preventing any chance of a clear picture.

The comedy continued as the quartet climbed back into the car and drove into the car park of the prison, Charlie lying on the rear seat. When finally the wicket gate opened and a prison officer appeared, the red Cortina drove at full speed right up to the gates, Charlie dived out of the car and went into the nick like a scalded cat and the performance was over. Leaving behind them a gaggle of fuming pressmen, Joey and his companions sped away on the road to London.

'What's the joke?' said Freddie Murphy.

Joey, still smiling, turned to his questioner.

'Just thinking of something funny,' he said.

Adgie was at his side. 'Just been talking to a couple of the lads,' he said in a low voice. 'They've had a whisper about the Cable Street mob. Come and have a word.'

'Sure,' said Joey. He turned to Murphy.

'Bit of business,' he said. 'Nice to see you. Regards to Charlie and Eddie when you see them.' He turned to Adgie.

'Lead the way,' he said.

6. Kill or be Killed

Within a few minutes' walk of Kensington Palace, and served by two tube stations, lies the thoroughfare known as Queensway. Extending from the Bayswater Road to Westbourne Grove it is a hive of multi-racial noise and bustle. During the hours of daylight the expensive boutiques and jewellery shops cater for well-heeled patrons of all nationalities, but it is at night that the street takes on a cosmopolitan atmosphere. In the lush surroundings of the casino thousands of pounds are won and lost. A bewildering variety of restaurants spread their appetising odours – Greek, Italian, Chinese, Indian; all tastes can be satisfied in the course of a short exploratory stroll.

Joey's favourite Indian restaurant was situated towards the Bayswater Road end of the street, and it was there that the taxi set him and Francesca down at about nine thirty in the evening. As they were ushered to a table in the centre of the room, Francesca sniffed appreciatively.

'If the smell's anything to go by I'm going to enjoy this meal,' she said.

'I think you will, Duchess,' said Joey. 'The tandoori chicken is out of this world.'

The words were hardly out of his mouth when the door of the restaurant crashed back on its hinges. Framed in the opening was the menacing figure of Hippie Palmer, flourishing a nine-inch blade. Close on his heels was the gigantic Basher James, his right fist closed round an iron bar. Sidling into the room, bent almost double and stiletto at the ready, Spanish Pete moved into a flanking position. For a matter of seconds there was a silence in which the dropping of a pin would have made a considerable racket.

'Heads up, Duchess. It's on top,' Joey shouted.

Francesca's hands went to the pockets of the light coat, her fingers slipping into the brass knuckles. As Palmer screamed, a high-pitched ululating animal howl, her right foot flashed out and impacted on his groin. The howl turned into a roar of pure agony and, as her victim's knees buckled, the brass knuckles flashed as a right and left thudded to either side of his head. Palmer was out. She turned her attention to the hulking Basher James.

Spanish Pete had concentrated on Joey, mounting what he fondly imagined to be a surprise attack on the flank. As he lunged with the stiletto, Joey moved inside the blow and, seizing his assailant by the lapels of his jacket, butted him in the middle of his face. There was a satisfying crack and a spurt of claret as the nose broke and, as the little Spaniard collapsed, Joey jumped in the air and came down with both feet on his opponent's kneecaps.

There was a sneer on the ugly face of Basher James as, swinging the iron bar, he moved in on the slight female form confronting him. Francesca, her teeth bared in a tigerish snarl, ducked under a clumsy attempt to disable her and beat a rapid tattoo with brass-knuckled fists on Basher's massive chest. As his ribs shattered, penetrating the lungs, Basher coughed and crimson rivulets spouted from the corners of his mouth. His knees gave way and, as he slowly sank to the floor, the brass knuckles flashed and gaping wounds sprang like red flowers from his cheeks and head.

The fight was over. The diners and staff were nowhere to be seen. Some had fought their way out of the door and into the street, others had sought refuge in the lavatories, some had vanished through the service door into the kitchens. Joey looked around him.

'We've got ten seconds, Duchess,' he said. 'Cripple 'em.'

Steel-shod feet crashed into the recumbent bodies. Coolly and scientifically Joey and Francesca ensured that their attackers would never walk upright again. As silence descended on the scene of carnage, the diners and the restaurant staff came slowly from their various places of refuge. The proprietor emerged from behind the bar. Francesca slipped the brass knuckles into her pockets and sat in an adjacent chair, not a hair out of place.

'Better send for an ambulance, Mumtaz,' said Joey.

'I have done that already,' said the proprietor somewhat stunned, and as he spoke the wail of a siren was heard sounding from the street outside.

The ambulance crew was quick to recognise an emergency. There were no questions asked as the bodies were quickly loaded onto stretchers and whisked away. The only comment came from the chief of the crew.

'The police will be along soon,' he said.

Soon was the operative word. Hardly had the ambulance siren faded into the distance than a patrol car drew up to the kerb and four uniformed officers ploughed their way through the crowd that was gathered round the restaurant entrance. The sergeant in charge entered warily, followed by two constables. Their colleague stayed outside to clear the street of the crowd of onlookers blocking the pavement.

Seeing that all was quiet, the sergeant removed his cap, and the two constables followed suit. Casting a wary eye around, the sergeant's glance alighted on a familiar face. He walked straight over to Joey.

'Could we have a word, sir?' he said.

'Of course,' said Joey. He led the way to the rear of the room, where the two men faced each other.

'What's all this about, Joey?' said the sergeant.

'Nothing much, Andy. Me and my partner were about to sit down to dinner. She's over there, by the way. You can speak to her later if you want to. Anyway, these three fellows barge in, all tooled up, and have a pop at us. Course we defend ourselves and they get hurt. The ambulance takes them away and that's it.'

Joey and Andy had been brought up on the same patch. Andy had joined the forces of law and order, Joey had become a villain. They both knew the score.

'That's all there is to it, Joey?' said Andy. 'Just a fight in a restaurant?'

'That's all.'

Andy called to the two officers who lingered near the entrance.

'All right, Jones, Henderson. Wait for me in the car. I'll clear up here.'

He turned to Joey. 'I hear you're doing well,' he said.

'Yes. By the way, here's my card. Just in case somebody wants to see me.'

'That's quite likely,' said Andy. 'If I know you, these geezers will be suffering more than slight bruising. Anyway, I'll put in my report, then it's out of my hands.'

'Thanks, Andy. See you around, eh?'

'We'll have a drink one evening – when I'm off duty.'

The restaurant was returning to normal when Joey rejoined Francesca.

'Still fancy tandoori chicken, Duchess?' he said.

'Let's eat,' she replied. 'Exercise always makes me ravenous.'

In the intensive care unit of the local hospital the latest entrants were being prepared for surgery. After a careful inspection of the three unconscious bodies the surgeon turned to the staff nurse.

'What happened to these men?' he said.

'Admissions say they were involved in a fight. An Indian restaurant in Queensway.'

The surgeon possessed a wry sense of humour.

'Now what would they be doing with a concrete mixer in an Indian restaurant?' he said.

'Pardon, sir?'

'Multiple lacerations, broken ribs, fractured limbs, severe head injuries. Consistent with being fed through a concrete mixer.' He indicated the supine body of what had once been Spanish Pete. 'We can forget about this one. Concentrate on saving the other two. The theatre ready?'

'Yes, sir.'

'Right. Let's get on with it.'

★

Francesca leaned against the parallel bars and watched Joey as he ended a session on the heavy bag. As usual, she was wearing only the tiny briefs which barely covered her sex.

'I'd like a word with you, partner,' she said.

Joey stripped off the light leather gloves and placed them neatly on a shelf nearby.

'Go ahead,' he said.

'You knew it was going to be off at the restaurant last night, didn't you?'

'Correction. I knew it was going to be off. I didn't know when.'

'That's why you insisted on the knuckles and the special shoes. Right?'

'Right.'

'Why didn't you put me in the picture?'

Joey chose his words carefully. 'Well,' he said, 'I couldn't tell you what I didn't know. Then again, you should have got the message when I told you not to forget your equipment. Anyway, what's the odds. You put on a first-class performance. How did you enjoy it?'

Francesca's lips curled in a vicious grin. 'It was over too soon,' she said. 'But I must say, I was surprised they picked such a public place as a restaurant. Why didn't they wait until later and try and get us in some dark alley or other?'

'The surprise element, Duchess,' said Joey. 'Always do the last thing people would expect.'

'I could have killed those bastards.'

'Maybe you did,' said Joey. 'You're a bloodthirsty little sod. Wonder where you'll go from here. Now that you've tasted blood, I mean.'

'On to the next victory.'

'Go and get showered before you catch a cold,' said Joey. 'We'll continue the chat upstairs.'

Over coffee in his sitting room, Joey gave a brief outline of the events of the previous day.

'Adgie told me he had a whisper that there was a contract out on me,' he said. 'We popped down the Dale to see what we could find out. A couple of the hounds confirmed it, so I knew I could expect trouble.'

'Who's put out the contract?' asked Francesca.

'I have my suspicions. Can't prove anything. They had a pop at me before I left England. They'll try again, make no mistake.' There was a note of savagery in his voice as he went on. 'I'll nail the bastards sooner or later, Duchess. You can bet on it.'

'What's at the bottom of all this, Joey,' she said. 'Who are they, and what have you got that makes you a danger to them?'

'I guess you'll have to know sometime. Well, there's a vice ring that involves a lot of top people. I've got very incriminating tapes on some of their doings. They're well protected. I'm going to bring them down. They've been responsible for any number of murders . . .'

'But how did you get involved?'

'They tried to pin the killings on me.'

'So. Now I get the picture. This is what the feud is about. Revenge.'

'Yes.'

There was a pregnant silence. For his part, Joey wondered how much his partner knew and whether it would be wise to involve her in what he thought of as his own private war. He was quickly made aware that he could not keep her out of it. She shot a question at him.

'Does the name Matthew Gill mean anything to you?'

Her eyes searched his face as he considered his answer.

'What do you know about Gill?' he countered.

'Joey, I'm a bright girl and I get around. Everybody knows that Gill is kinky. I've heard stories about his parties. There's a silly old prick I know, loves being sucked off by little girls. I sat next to him at a dinner party once. He was trying to grope me under the table. He got well pissed and started to boast about how he'd been to one of Gill's parties. I suppose he thought he'd turn me on, told me about being gammed by a kid with a suction like a Hoover. Silly old fart. In fact, he's invited me to one of these parties next week.'

Joey mentioned a name that was a household word. 'That the fellow?' he said.

'That's him. How did you guess?'

'No guessing. He's on one of the tapes.'

Francesca sat in shocked silence. 'Bloody Nora,' she said. 'How many more famous faces have you got on these tapes?'

'Plenty,' said Joey grimly.

'Christ. No wonder they want you out of the way. When can I see these horror pictures?'

'No dice,' said Joey. 'You just stick to being my partner in J. Bello Investigations. Go to the party if you're that curious. The other is my private war, for the time being at any rate.'

Francesca smiled. 'Whatever you say, Joey,' she said. Privately she made a mental reservation. When the game was really on, she intended to be part of it.

The meetings between Finch and Gill were becoming more frequent. This time they came together in the latter's consulting rooms, where Gill was taking a quick sandwich lunch between appointments. A plentiful supply of smoked salmon in brown bread was laid out on a silver platter and a bottle of Moselle rested in a cooler. Gill picked up a sandwich and nibbled daintily.

'The forces of law and order defeated again, Finch?' he was saying. 'How the hell this fellow keeps getting away with it beats me. What happened this time?'

'I put in three hard men, real killers,' said Finch. 'They cornered Bello and the Smithson-Wright woman in a restaurant in Bayswater. The report on the incident is with my Serious Crimes Squad. It seems that Bello and the woman slaughtered my men. Two of them are in intensive care. They'll never walk again. The third one died shortly after arriving in hospital.'

'Jolly good,' said Gill. 'All you have to do now is to nick Bello, he's tried for murder, gets a life sentence and he's out of our hair.'

'Don't be stupid,' growled Finch. 'The report says that three men armed with offensive weapons made an unprovoked attack on two innocent people. There's a stack of witnesses. They all say that Bello and the woman defended themselves. On the facts as stated, the DPP would be a fool to prosecute. All Bello has to do in that case is to hire the best brief in the country, who'll tie the prosecution up in knots. They'll prove that the dead man had some organic defect or other which would render him liable to drop dead at any time, Bello and the woman would get medals for bravery, the costs would be met out of public funds and the police would be a laughing stock. Don't for Christ's sake give me any more of your simple solutions.'

Gill was nettled and showed it. 'The trouble with you, Finch, is that you're not much of a man and even less of a senior police officer. You're a crack shot, aren't you? Well, get hold of a sniper's rifle, see that Bello is lured to some quiet spot and put a bullet through his head from a safe distance. Dead easy, what?'

Finch made no secret of his exasperation.

'Dead easy my arse,' he said. 'You can't be serious. Do you suggest that a Commander in the Met could be personally implicated in the commission of a crime like murder? You must be off your rocker.'

'My dear Finch, you're suffering from delusions of grandeur,' said Gill. 'Your subordinates at the Yard lick your boots. Your slightest word is their command. Don't run away with the idea that you can behave in these consulting rooms as if you were in your office. So far as I'm concerned you are a Grammar-school-educated illiterate, a highly-placed yobbo whose main function is to protect me and my friends, for which you are well paid. Do I make myself clear?'

Finch's face darkened and a small vein pulsated in his temple. His anger was such that he almost lost the power of speech. When he finally spoke the words tumbled over each other.

'This whole situation is your fault. If you hadn't made those videotapes we wouldn't be in this mess . . .'

Gill interrupted, his voice cold and incisive. 'Shut up and listen to me. I can bring out big guns that will make your pitiful lot look like a gang of schoolboys armed with peashooters. Now get out of here and do the job you're paid for. Just remember this. You're only a lickspittle.'

Finch admitted defeat. Though trembling with rage, he managed to keep his voice under control.

'You've made your point, Gill. Bear in mind we're on the same side.'

It was a feeble parting shot which Gill did not deem worthy of a reply.

The Jaguar, Adgie at the wheel, turned off the motorway into a narrow country lane bordered by trees. The car was, as usual, gleaming but with one exception. The number plates, normally quite readable, appeared to have picked up some splashes of mud which partially obscured some of the letters and digits. Adgie, ever the complete professional, was not in the habit of neglecting detail.

Francesca and Joey occupied the rear seats. She was wearing a light coat covering her from neck to mid-calf and buttoned securely down the whole of its length. Joey presented a bizarre sight, clad in full Satan regalia, complete with horns and an evil mask that concealed all of his face with the exception of the chin. He wore a long black cloak reaching down to his ankles.

'Got the tickets, Duchess?' he asked.

'Right here,' she said, patting her coat pocket. She leaned forward in her seat, peering out of the window.

'Slow up, Adgie,' she said. 'Take the next on the left.'

Adgie touched the brake pedal then swung left into the entrance to a drive between two massive stone pillars. Though it was now dusk, the outlines of a large house were clearly defined against the darkening sky beyond a belt of low-lying shrubbery. At the end of the drive they came to a large circular area round which a number of expensive cars were parked. Adgie brought the car to a halt under a portico from which a short flight of steps led to the front door of the mansion.

Joey got out first, closely followed by Francesca.

'You know what to do,' said Joey to Adgie.

He received a nod in reply and the car slid away into the gathering darkness.

They mounted the steps to the door and Francesca placed a finger on the bell-push. The response was almost immediate and a shaft of light from the hallway silhouetted a large man in a dinner jacket who stood aside to allow them to pass.

'May I see your invitations please?' he said.

Francesca handed him the two cards which he scrutinised closely.

'Thank you. Mr Smith and Miss Jones. Please go through.'

As they passed through a pair of secondary doors which led onto the hallway, Francesca slipped on a tiny mask. On the other side of the portals they halted for a moment and looked around them at an astonishing sight. The party was evidently in full swing. Almost directly before them a naked girl leaned on a stout table as a young man mounted her vigorously from the rear. On the steps of the huge stairway which led to the upper part of the house were three more couples in various attitudes but with a common purpose which could best be described as acrobatic copulation.

A young man emerged from a side room. He wore a Roman toga and a broad smile and moved in a cloud of musky perfume.

'Your upper and outer garments please,' he said. He reached for Joey's cloak.

'I'll keep it on. Part of the costume,' said Joey.

'Dearie me,' lisped the young man. 'What have we got to hide then?'

He made a determined grab for Joey's genitalia which was just as determinedly repulsed.

'Naughty, naughty. You'll have to unmask at midnight, you know,' he said.

He turned to Francesca who slipped out of her coat and handed it to him. Joey had to bite his lip to restrain a burst of laughter. Apart from a tiny scrap of material in the shape of a leaf which was stuck to her pubic hair with some sort of adhesive, she was completely naked. The young man gave a delighted squeal.

'Ooh! Eve from the Garden of Eden. I hope you meet your Adam, dear.'

She flashed him a brilliant smile.

'Well, it won't be you, will it?' she said.

'I'm afraid not.' He waved a languid hand. 'I haven't got that kind of equipment. Do go in. The main hall's over there. Good fucking, darling.'

As they moved away from the still-smiling youth, Joey took Francesca's arm.

'Tempting Providence a bit, aren't you?' he said.

'No way. You know that anybody who tries to get into my palmers is on a losing wicket.'

'Just a prick-tease is it?'

'You could say that. Come on. Let's see what's on offer.'

They passed through into the main hall, an enormous room where the curtains of the many large windows were firmly drawn. Two massive crystal chandeliers shed their light on a scene that was beyond description. About thirty men and women of varying ages were either lounging on settees which were dotted about the room, lying on cushions on the floor or standing in small groups apparently deep in conversation. They had one thing in common. All were engaged in some form of sexual activity.

A group of three standing by the fireplace caught Joey's eye. The woman was between the two men holding a penis in each hand, which she fondled and caressed almost absent-mindedly. One of the men had thrust his hand into the cleft of her buttocks and was making massaging movements. Had they been wearing clothes and holding drinks in their hands they could have been guests at a country house party.

A short and corpulent old man was padding round the room carrying a tray laden with glasses of champagne. He was one of the few not wearing a mask and was in the semi-nude, a small cotton apron hiding his genitals. Joey recognised the face at once.

'Jesus,' he said. 'You know who that is?'

'Yes. That's my silly old fart. The one who provided the tickets. Get ready for laughs when he spots me.'

They did not have long to wait. The silly old fart was making a beeline for Francesca. He came up to her, panting, tiny slivers of spittle at the corners of his mouth.

'Darling,' he quavered. 'I didn't think you'd turn up.' He ignored Joey as though he were a piece of furniture.

'Well, here I am,' said Francesca.

'Are you going to suck me off tonight?'

'I'll see how I feel. If I'm in the mood,' she said, groaning inwardly with revulsion.

'I hope so. Now you must excuse me. I have customers.'

Joey watched the drooping backside as the ancient pervert left them. He was not a sentimental man, but he felt a touch of pity as the old fellow circulated among his more juvenile clientele. He was treated with scant courtesy and subjected to a certain amount of humiliation, yet he seemed to enjoy it. As he handed a glass of champagne to a hirsute middle-aged man who was tickling the tonsils of a blowsy blonde with a half-erect organ, he received a kick in the crotch. Joey distinctly heard him say 'Thank you for the tip, sir'.

The air was heavy with the reek of cannabis and in one corner of the room a small queue was waiting patiently to sniff lines of cocaine prepared by a public-spirited benefactor. Looking around him, Joey recognised many well-known faces who, amazingly enough, were prepared to risk their reputations for an evening of sexual gratification. He turned to Francesca, who was being chatted up by an almost inarticulate character who retained a semblance of dignity by wearing a pair of boxer shorts.

'Going to take a look round upstairs, Duchess,' he said.

'Go ahead,' she replied. 'You know where to find me.'

He negotiated the loving couples on the stairs and came to the first floor landing where he was confronted by a number of doors behind which, he had no doubt, there were all sorts of goings-on. Cautiously he opened the first door he came to and peered through the crack. In the dimly-lit room he discerned the naked body of a man lying on his back, his legs outspread. A female figure was crouched between his knees, her head moving rhythmically up and down. Standing athwart his head a black girl spurted her urine into his face as he made swallowing noises. Bottoms up, said Joey to himself as he softly closed the door.

The next room was unoccupied, but a further door opened to reveal a spectacle which, had it not had its tragic undertones, would have been comic. In the centre of the room stood a grotesquely fat woman with sagging breasts and a bulging abdomen. Her flabby body was decorated with clothes pegs pinching the surplus flesh. Around her stood three men, all middle-aged, their eyes bulging as they masturbated, jerking away as though their lives depended on their exertions. As Joey watched, one of them ejaculated, spattering the woman's body with semen.

Joey did not know whether to laugh or cry, so he did neither, moving further down the corridor and trying the doors of the many rooms he passed. All were unoccupied with the exception of the final one. Standing outside, he heard muffled screams coming from within, which reached a crescendo as he pushed the door slightly open and looked inside.

He took in the scene at a glance. In the centre of the floor was the only piece of furniture the room contained, a hospital-type bed on which lay the naked body of a young woman. Her wrists and ankles were firmly secured by leather straps to the framework of the bed and there was a gag in her mouth. Over her stood the menacing figure of a man wielding a riding crop which he brought down with considerable force over and over again on the buttocks and legs of his victim. The man was wearing only a gaily-coloured sarong, but Joey recognised him at once. The last time he had seen him was in a Harley Street consulting room.

Matthew Gill was so engrossed in his task that he would not have noticed if a bomb had exploded beside him. A look of animal ferocity on his face, he struck the helpless body before him repeatedly. Each time the crop descended it was followed by a convulsive jerk as the woman strained against her bonds. Now she was making small moaning sounds through the gag as the crop cut into her flesh and blood began to flow freely, but the savage beating went on. At last there was no more movement and the moaning stopped.

What followed made Joey's blood run cold. Gill threw off the sarong and, penis rampant, hurled himself on to the woman's unconscious form, entering her with one swift lunge and voluptuously squirming on the bloody back in a welter of gore. He pumped away, slowly at first but increasing the tempo as he neared his climax.

Joey had seen enough. Without even going to the trouble of closing the door, he turned and made his way down the corridor to the other part of the first floor that lay beyond the head of the stairs. Now he abandoned caution and passed swiftly down the corridor, opening and closing doors at random. One room provided him with a strange sight. In a high chair sat a slender child who, to judge by her immature body and small breasts, had only recently passed her sixteenth birthday. She sucked on a dummy teat as a stout, bald-headed man probed the cleft between her outspread legs with his tongue as he, in turn, was buggered by an athletic young fellow who looked as though he was capable of maintaining an erection for ever and a day.

'Come and join us,' said the young man gaily, not pausing in his stroke. The other man had his mouth full.

'Thanks. Later perhaps,' said Joey as he made a rapid exit.

Out in the corridor a naked young woman bumped into him. She was stoned out of her mind. As she staggered and almost fell, Joey put a restraining arm round her. With a shriek of delight she pressed herself against him.

'Mephistopheles. My lord of evil. Rape me. Degrade me. I am your slave.'

'Not tonight, Josephine,' he said. He suddenly felt that he wanted to be out of this house. He disengaged himself none too gently and she slipped to the floor. As he retraced his steps to the head of the stairs, her plaintive cries followed him as she gave vent to a stream of obscenities.

Down in the hallway a minor fracas was under way. A naked Gill, still smeared with the blood of his recent victim, had evidently decided that he would like another helping, and had picked on Francesca as a suitable candidate. Now he had taken her by the arm, trying to pull her towards the stairway. From his point of vantage, where he could see without being seen, Joey allowed himself a smug satisfied smile. Any minute now and Gill wouldn't know what had hit him.

Gill now made the serious mistake of putting his hands on Francesca's shoulders in an attempt to swing her round and propel her towards the stairs. Her hands came up to break the hold and, as Gill fell back, her knee went up and drove accurately into his crotch. Screaming with pain Gill reeled into the massive newel supporting the banister and Francesca moved in to finish the job.

The noise brought the burly doorman to the scene. He was followed by an equally large and tough-looking character and together they moved purposefully towards Francesca. It was then that the Devil took a hand in the game. Letting out a loud and nerve-shattering roar Joey flew down the stairs and tore into the two men, fists and feet flying. They hit the deck and stayed there.

'Come on, Duchess. Have it away,' Joey yelled.

'My coat,' cried Francesca.

'Sod your coat. Come on.'

Side by side they catapulted through the main door and down the steps to the drive. Adgie must have had the engine of the Jag running, for within seconds the car, headlights blazing, rear door swinging open, sped towards them. As Adgie momentarily slowed, Joey and Francesca tumbled in. Adgie put his foot down and within seconds they were through the gates at the end of the drive and onto the narrow country lane that led to the motorway.

Joey removed his mask and passed it to Francesca.

'Here, put this on,' he said. 'You must be a bit chilly.'

The late afternoon sun flooded the sitting room of Joey's private apartment. Clad in bath robe and slippers, Joey was perusing the documentation on the Macowan case. Lurking in the back of his mind was the feeling that, somewhere among the reports and the transcripts of telephone conversations, he would find some reference to the problem that was occupying his mind to the exclusion of everything else. Was Macowan connected in any way with the Gill conspiracy? He was forced to the conclusion that no such connection existed.

The internal telephone shrilled and he lifted the handset.

'There's a Chief Superintendent Duval at the door, sir,' came Marion's voice.

'Just a minute.' Joey clicked a switch and the screen on the wall came to life. He recognised the man immediately. It was indeed the Detective Chief Superintendent.*

'I've got him on picture,' said Joey. 'Give him the usual spiel. I'll monitor it.'

Marion's voice as she spoke to the caller was clear and unflurried.

'Do you have a warrant, sir?' she said.

'No,' came the reply.

'Then I'm afraid you will have to telephone or write for an appointment. Mr Bello is not available to casual callers.'

'Very well. Can you give me a number?'

*See BORN ROTTEN by the same author.

'Certainly, sir. You may ring at any time.' She gave him a telephone number which he scrawled on his palm with a ball-point pen. He turned his back and mingled with the pedestrians on the pavement of Park Lane.

Joey spoke to Marion. 'We'll have a call within the next five minutes,' he said. 'Put him straight through.'

When Duval spoke to Joey it was without preamble.

'I'd like a word,' he said. 'Can I come round?'

Joey was equally brusque. 'No,' he said.

'It's unofficial. Off the record.'

'Where are you?' said Joey.

'In the lounge at the Cumberland.'

'I'll be with you in ten minutes.'

It was exactly ten minutes later that Joey walked into the lounge of the Cumberland Hotel. He wore informal clothes, a tiny tape recorder lodged in the breast pocket of his jacket.

Duval rose to meet him, holding out a hand, which Joey shook perfunctorily.

'We'll just visit the toilet,' he said.

'I'm not wired up, if that's what you think,' said Duval.

'Then you won't mind if I check,' replied Joey.

The toilet was deserted. Joey gave Duval a quick rub-down. The man had told the truth.

'What's on your mind?' asked Joey.

'Let's find a quiet table and have a word.'

Returning to the lounge, Duval led the way to a deserted corner. In a quiet voice he began to speak.

'First of all, I want to make it clear that this meeting is off the record,' he said.

'I'll make it clear too,' said Joey. 'In my book all coppers are bastards. The last time we had anything to do with each other, you left me in the shit with your Commander's gang of murderers after me. I was lucky to get away alive.'

'I found that out later,' said Duval. 'Believe me, I'm truly sorry. There was nothing I could do at the time. Now the situation's different. Commander Finch is under internal investigation.' There was passion in his voice as he went on. 'Joey, I hate bent coppers. I saw those tapes. You can help me. I want that filthy bastard out of the force.'

'All right, Duval . . .'

'The name's John,' interrupted Duval.

'Very well . . . John,' said Joey. 'Let's have it.'

'I'm now in charge of Serious Crime,' said Duval. 'I have a report on my desk about an affray in an Indian restaurant in Bayswater. Three men with records of violent crime made an unprovoked attack on Joseph Bello, a private enquiry agent, and his partner, a Miss Francesca Smithson-Wright. The assailants were armed with offensive weapons, and the victims were obliged to use considerable force to defend themselves. One man died and the other two suffered serious injuries. My report to the DPP will recommend no further action be taken.'

'Very wise,' said Joey. 'I'm not bothered. That's one I would have walked away from.'

'I know. Look. Will you tell me what you know about who is behind this whole business?'

'Not bloody likely,' replied Joey. 'When the time comes for an official enquiry yours truly will be there. Till then me and my partner are well able to take care of ourselves. You look out for yourself. If the top brass close ranks behind Finch you'll be well and truly fucked, just like you were before.'

Duval knew when he was defeated. From previous experience he was aware of the dangers of concerted action by superior officers which could destroy even Chief Superintendents. Nevertheless he did not give up.

'Have you got copies of those videotapes, Joey?'

'I might have. Then again, I might not.'

'If you do have them, would you be prepared to hand them over to me?'

'Not on your Nellie,' replied Joey. 'They're my trump card. They stay up my sleeve.'

'Well, if you ever need my help, let me know.'

Joey laughed. 'What makes you think I'd welcome your

performing monkeys dancing on my patch. Be your age, John. One bent bastard, even a lowly constable, could put the kybosh on you. All right, you're a straight copper, but you're surrounded by a bunch of official villains who'd grass you up as soon as look at you.'

Duval shook his head sadly. 'I suppose you're right, Joey. It's a bad reflection on our society that a statement like that can go unchallenged, even by me.'

'They're facts of life. I've learned them the hard way,' said Joey. 'Anyway, bugger philosophy. It's dog eat dog in the world we live in.'

'I can't disagree with you. You've done your share of bird, you've seen injustice at first hand. But take the Kray twins, for example. What's your point of view?'

'Well, there it was kill or be killed. When villains do away with other villains it saves you a lot of paperwork and does society a favour. That's realism.'

'Or is it anarchy,' said Duval.

'Take your pick. Who's going to be the judge? The twins are stuck away for life or thirty years, whichever is the shortest. They have to watch child-molesters go out on parole and then see them come back inside again after they've ruined some other kid's life. You're the lawman. You tell me.'

John Duval was a decent man with a sense of family, loved by his wife and two teenage daughters. He did his job conscientiously, was respected by his subordinates and only rarely earned the disapproval of his superiors. He had always believed that questions of law were best decided by jurists. His faith in that direction had been shaken when he witnessed the public humiliation of the upholders of law and order branded by the press as sexual perverts. Now, talking on terms of easy familiarity with a man who had been treated as an enemy of society, he was on uncertain ground.

'We've got to do the best we can,' he said, and realised the lameness of his argument even as he uttered the words.

'Come off it, John. Are you trying to tell me that a wise

and upright interpreter of the law who writes odes to small boys' arseholes is a fit and proper person to direct a jury in a case of multiple rape? You know the answer is bollocks.'

'Point taken, Joey.' Duval glanced at his watch. 'Let's postpone our discussion. I'm due at the Yard in ten minutes.'

'See you later,' said Joey. 'You leave first. It won't do either of us any good to be seen leaving here together.'

Duval left the hotel, and Joey followed after a few minutes. Their departure was observed by a burly individual who seemed to spend most of his time hidden behind a newspaper held close to his face.

Mention the Yard to any member of the criminal fraternity and he will know exactly what you mean. Once upon a time it was Scotland Yard, a warren of buildings within a stone's throw of the Mother of Parliaments. Now the headquarters of the Metropolitan Police are situated in a vast building in Westminster and, in case there are any doubts in the minds of the public as to what goes on within its portals, a revolving sign at the imposing entrance blazons in large letters the words NEW SCOTLAND YARD.

From this building the Commissioner of Police for the Metropolis, through a network of Assistant Commissioners, Deputy Assistant Commissioners and Commanders, controlled the policing of Greater London. His position was one of tremendous power which carried with it an equally onerous responsibility. The prevention of crime was his main task but, once a crime had been committed, it was his job also to ensure that the criminal was apprehended. Punishment could be left to the Courts.

Commander Finch enjoyed a special position in the hierarchy at the Yard. He was possessed of a roving commission which gave him the right to monitor investigations into large-scale criminal activities ranging from the traffic in drugs to high-level fraud. This afternoon he was closeted with the head of the Serious Crimes Squad, Detective Chief Superintendent John Duval.

Finch had adopted an attitude of cheerful bonhomie when Duval entered his office.

'Come in and sit down, John,' he said. 'How are you getting on in Serious Crimes?'

'Very well thank you, sir. No complaints.'

'Good. I'd like a word about a little matter that's cropped up. Man called Bello. You remember him?'

'Vaguely, sir. Wasn't he supposed to have stolen some videotapes? I do remember that you took over the investigation.'

'Quite correct, John. Bello skipped the country. Now he's back again. Plenty of money. Set up a private enquiry business. Very up-market.'

Duval had had experience of the Commander's devious ways.

'I've just put in a report about him, sir,' he said. 'An affray in a restaurant. Three armed men attacked Bello and a lady companion. One of the attackers died in hospital.'

'Yes, John. I've seen a copy of your report. You recommend no further action. Why?'

'I thought that would be obvious, sir. On the evidence, no jury would convict.'

'I quite agree. But tell me, what's your honest opinion of this man?'

'I'm a copper, he's a villain. A reformed villain, true. As long as he tows the line he's safe. Let him commit a crime and I'll be on him like a ton of bricks.'

Finch rubbed his chin reflectively. 'I don't know the ins and outs of it,' he said. 'Any idea who might have had it in for Bello?'

'Not really, sir. Bello's a villain from way back. He must have made many enemies. Probably somebody settling a few scores.'

'Yes. That figures. Still, I don't fancy this fellow being at large, going round killing people. Couldn't – er – something be done?'

Finch's intention was now quite clear to his subordinate. It was an open indication that the Commander would be quite happy to see Joey Bello fitted up on some serious charge or other and whisked away for a long sojourn as a guest of Her Majesty. Duval decided to play stupid.

'What do you suggest, sir?' he said.

'Well, I really don't quite know. Let's say Bello's place was raided and a large quantity of heroin was found on the premises? You see what I mean?'

Christ, thought Duval, the man must have lost his marbles. Or else he was desperate. Even to mention such a course of action amounted to professional suicide if the facts ever came out. Duval was aware of the cloud of suspicion over the Commander's head. He was equally aware that suspicion was one thing but proof was another. He put on a vacant look.

'I don't think Bello would be stupid enough to push drugs,' he said. 'You say he has plenty of money . . .'

'So where does he get it from?' interrupted Finch.

'Yes, sir, I see what you mean. But how can we be sure that Bello will have the stuff on the premises?'

Finch called a halt to the verbal fencing. It was now evident that Duval was being deliberately obtuse. No further risks could be taken. Convinced that Duval would not play ball in an attempt to fit up his intended victim, Finch switched the attack.

'Yes. That's a consideration,' he said. 'What about the woman. His partner. Have we anything on her?'

'She's as clean as a whistle. Very respectable and well-connected. Father's a QC. Mother's a successful writer. No chance there.'

'Peculiar set-up, don't you think?'

Duval maintained his obdurate stance.

'I'm a police officer not a psychologist, sir,' he said.

Finch realised he was getting nowhere.

'All right, John,' he said. 'Thanks for coming up. Will you keep me advised of developments?'

'Certainly, sir.'

The interview was concluded. On the way back to his office Duval realised he now possessed vital information which, when the time was ripe, could be used in bringing about the downfall of a man who, in his book, merited only contempt. Softly, softly catchee monkey, he murmured under his breath, and was still smiling as he turned the handle of his office door.

Francesca Smithson-Wright could not remember the last time she had been so completely satisfied with life. That morning she had had a strenuous work-out in the gym at the house in Park Lane and her body was tingling with the after-effects. She had left a message with Marion that she would be at her flat, and was now busily preparing the kind of snack that no restaurant would be able to provide.

In her private moments she invariably went about stark naked. She loved the feeling of soft carpet beneath her bare feet, the complete freedom when her movements were unfettered by hampering garments. Now, standing over the electric stove in her well-equipped kitchen, she was completely at ease.

The simple dish which she was preparing was a cheese omelette made exactly to her taste. The coffee machine was already perfuming the air with the fragrance of her favourite dark-roasted Moroccan bean, the golden toast in the rack on the table. She tossed a chunk of unsalted butter into the hot omelette pan, which was never washed but only wiped out after use, waited a few moments then added the three eggs which had been lightly whisked and anointed with salt and freshly-ground pepper. As she forked the cooked edges of the mixture towards the centre of the pan she sprinkled a liberal helping of Parmesan cheese over the semi-liquid surface, deftly flipped over the edges, changed her grip on the pan and slid on to a warm plate the perfect omelette. The whole operation had taken less than three minutes.

She was wiping her plate with the last remnants of the toast when the telephone rang. She lifted the handset.

'Morning, Duchess,' said Joey. As usual, he made the conversation short and to the point. 'Fancy a trip to Parkhurst tomorrow?'

'I'd love it,' she replied.

'Fine. We'll go in your car. Get a bit of fresh air. Pick me up at half-nine, OK?'

'I'll be there,' she said.

The flame-red Alfa-Romeo, hood down, sped along the Kingston by-pass at a sedate seventy miles an hour. Although it was late August, it was a bright morning. The blue sky was flecked with a few streaks of cirrus cloud, giving promise of a fine day to come. Joey put his companion in the picture.

'An old mate wants to see me,' he said. 'Name's Freddie Bates. He's doing fifteen for armed robbery. Don't know what it's about.'

'We'll find out when we get there,' said Francesca. 'In the meantime, let's enjoy the trip. Which way shall we go? Motorway or the old Portsmouth Road?'

'The old road for me. Motorways are for morons, Duchess, not for us.'

Francesca put her foot down. Esher, Guildford, the Devil's Punch Bowl and Hindhead were left behind in the thin blue smoke from the Alfa's twin exhausts. They stopped for coffee and a sandwich at an ancient hostelry in Liphook, then pressed on to the summit of Portsmouth Hill where they were able to look down on the harbour and the broad waters of the Solent beyond. Then it was on down to the city proper and embarkation on to the ferry that would take them to Cowes on the Isle of Wight.

They drew into the visitors' car park at Parkhurst shortly before two o'clock. Alighting from the car, Francesca stood for a few moments surveying the grim walls which, even in the sunlight of a bright summer's day, looked grey and forbidding.

'How long were you inside there?' she asked.

'Six years,' Joey replied.

She made no comment. At the gate Joey produced the Visiting Order which was their permit to enter, and the pair were shown into a waiting room packed with a collection of characters of all sizes, shapes, sexes and colours. Joey paid little attention to the surroundings. Francesca, on the contrary, betrayed an avid interest in the incongruous mob, her eyes bright with curiosity as she looked around her. She, too, did not escape notice. Although she had dressed soberly for the occasion, she stood out, to use Joey's expressive phraseology, like a diamond in a heap of shit.

They were not kept long in the waiting room. Freddie Bates, as a Category A inmate, rated a certain priority which included open visits in a private room. Joey and Francesca followed the screw who led them up an outside stairway and into a fairly spacious area furnished in shiny chrome and formica and decently carpeted. The walls were distempered in pale blue and sported a few cheerful prints. As they took their seats at one of the tables, Francesca leaned towards Joey.

'Neat but not gaudy,' she said.

The three screws standing together in a far corner seemed to pay little attention to the visitors apart from a few sidelong glances. Francesca raised her eyebrows and Joey replied to the unspoken question.

'They don't miss much. Watch what you say,' he said in a low voice.

When Freddie Bates came into the room the two rose to their feet. Joey shook Freddie's hand.

'Freddie Bates – the Duchess,' he said by way of introduction.

Bates was a stockily-built man in his middle forties. His status in the prison hierarchy was evidenced by his uniform. The blue pullover was almost new and his neatly-pressed trousers were a perfect fit. Though Francesca would not have known it, the highly polished shoes were the pick of the establishment's shoemaking department.

It was obviously by prior arrangement that tea was

provided. One of the screws came to the table carrying a tray on which reposed a pot of tea, three cups, milk, sugar and a plate of biscuits. Francesca turned on her most radiant smile.

'That's very sweet of you. Thank you so much,' she said. Slightly weak at the knees, the screw returned her smile and retreated.

There followed a period of desultory conversation between Joey and Bates in which Francesca took no part. It was only when Joey asked the crucial question that she was all ears.

'So, what's it all about?' said Joey.

'Remember my boy?' said Bates.

'Sure. Young Freddie. Must be, what, nineteen, twenty . . .'

'Nineteen. He's dead.' Bates was on the verge of tears. Joey, who regarded death as no more than a serious accident, fell silent.

'He was on heroin,' said Bates. 'Her indoors told me nothing. Probably thought I would go over the wall.'

'I'm sorry,' said Joey, and realised the inadequacy of the words as soon as he had uttered them.

Then the tears came. Joey and Francesca sat in embarrassed silence. Finally Bates regained his composure. He wiped the sleeve of his pullover across his face. He spoke quietly but there was death in his voice.

'Joey, you owe me. I want the fuckers seen off. The same way my boy went. Promise me. You'll go and see the missus. Will you do that?'

'I will,' said Joey.

'Thanks,' said Bates. He got to his feet and walked back through the door by which he had entered. The visit was over.

There were no words exchanged between Joey and his partner until they were standing at the bar on the ferry. Joey had ordered large brandies. It was Francesca who broke the silence.

'What did he mean when he said you owed him?' she asked.

'He got me out of trouble once,' said Joey. 'He could have been killed himself. He was hurt – bad.'

'A life for a life,' said Francesca.

'That's the way it goes, Duchess.'

'What are you going to do?'

'First off I'll see his missus. Then I'll go on from there. If I don't do something he'll go over the wall and do it himself. That way he'll get life. You see what I mean?'

'I see exactly what you mean, Joey,' she said. 'Whatever you decide to do, count me in.'

Joey smiled grimly. 'It'll be rough,' he said.

She returned the smile and raised her glass.

'Don't forget I've tasted blood,' she said.

7. *The Wages of Sin*

There was a time when the smoking of cannabis, commonly referred to as shit or pot, was confined to wealthy socialites, jazz musicians and pop groups. Rastafarians regarded the habit as part of their religious rituals. Pressure groups agitated for the legalisation of what they called a harmless weed while the young, ever avid for new experience, smoked their joints and opened the doors to a perception of life beyond the boundaries of their imagination.

For those who wished to widen their horizons and venture further into the esoteric where reality gave way to hallucination, the answer lay in cocaine and heroin. In the Andes, Bolivia and Peru the coca bush grows in wild profusion and its leaves provide the raw material from which cocaine is extracted. The poppy that blooms in Flanders' fields also proliferates in places as far apart as Pakistan and Thailand. From the seeds of this red symbol of remembrance is processed the white powder known as heroin, skag or smack.

Cocaine, commonly referred to as coke, may be either sniffed or smoked. Sniffing is a somewhat inelegant procedure which involves chopping up the crystals of the drug with a razor blade and laying out two 'lines', one for each nostril. The 'lines' are then inhaled through a straw or a rolled-up banknote in a process known as snorting. Smoking is a less complicated and altogether more genteel business. A suitable pipe is stuffed with the drug, a light is applied and the proceeds of combustion drawn down into the lungs. Snorting or smoking, the end result is the same. In the higher centres of the brain something happens and the user is transported to a Nirvana of transcendental bliss, where the cares and worries of life are blown away like clouds before the wind.

Smoking heroin, or chasing the dragon, involves a slightly different or varied technique. The heroin powder is sprinkled onto a piece of silver foil, a lighter is held under the foil and the resulting vapour is inhaled through a tube into the mouth. The real addict, however, is satisfied with nothing less than a direct injection of a heroin solution into a vein by means of a hypodermic needle. The result is amazing, the consequence tragic. Sometimes, when the same needle is shared by two or more addicts, a blood condition may be transferred from one to the other. There is evidence to show that this practice has led in many cases to the spread of the virus of the killer disease AIDS.

Where a demand exists in our acquisitive society there will always be a supplier ready and willing to meet it. Drug abuse is widespread and increasing. Schoolchildren are being drawn into the drug-pusher's net, the young unemployed, bored by inactivity, fall victim to the new craze and take to crime in order to support their habit. What the authorities coyly refer to as 'illegal substances' flood into the Western world in ever-increasing quantities. The seizure rate by police and Customs cannot be defined exactly, but official estimates put it as low as five per cent.

The situation is ready-made for criminal elements to step in and take a hand in this lucrative business. Profits are astronomical and the risk almost negligible. By the time a kilo of cannabis, coke or smack has reached its user, it has multiplied in value at least six times. The unscrupulous dealer on the street will cut the already adulterated narcotic with a harmless powder which will serve to double or treble his profits. At the end of the chain of supply and distribution is a customer who must take what he is given because he is engaged in an illegal activity and therefore cannot complain.

The international criminal conspiracy known as the Mafia has had a hand in the organisation of the drug traffic for decades. With the massive funding derived from long-term involvement in vice and prostitution, backed by the laundered skim money from world-wide gambling operations, and with their guerilla army of desperadoes bound by the oath of 'omerta', death to the traitor, the Mafia are uniquely placed to suborn justice and corrupt the forces of law and order. Huge bribes can be offered to high-ranking officers in police forces in those countries where favours are granted on a strictly cash basis. The stubborn juror is tempted by the prospect of earning ten years' wages by the simple expedient of agreeing with his fellow jurymen. Even the most respectable members of the judiciary are not above accepting payment in kind to supplement their already luxurious life-styles.

At the centre of this putrescent mass of corruption is greed. Greed begets money, money begets power, power begets further greed until, in the last analysis, power is all. Pity and compassion are also-rans in the race for acquisition. If a million dollars equals fifty corpses, then so be it. Let the graves be dug. But let the coke-sniffers and heroin addicts think well on this, that the gratification of their desires is creating a canker in what we know as civilised society, which will in time destroy it.

Sitting opposite May Bates in the lounge of her small flat in the Dale, Joey listened intently to her story of what had happened to her son. Though only in her early forties, she looked nearer sixty. That she had once been a very handsome-looking girl was apparent. Now, worn down by twenty years as the wife of a villain, the mother of a newly-buried son, she was a pitiful spectacle.

'I didn't know what was happening,' she was saying. 'Young Freddie wasn't working. He'd come home in the early morning, sleep all day, then go off somewhere. He wouldn't tell me. I didn't know what to do, his Dad being away and all that. Then this happened.'

She burst into a storm of weeping, dabbing at her eyes with a sodden tissue. Joey waited stoically until she had regained her composure.

'They said it was a heroin overdose that killed him,' she went on. 'I didn't know . . . I didn't know.'

Joey reached forward and put a hand on her arm.

'Don't take on, May,' he said. 'Nothing will bring him back. I saw Freddie the other day. I promised him I would do something about what's happened.'

She took a fresh tissue from the box at her side and dried her eyes.

'I'd like to see the bastards dead,' she said savagely.

'Don't worry, May,' he said. 'I'll have 'em. You can lay odds on it. Look, have you got a recent photo of young Freddie?'

She got up and went to a small table against the wall, opened a drawer and took out a photograph which she handed to Joey. It showed a rather good-looking youth with smiling eyes but a hint of weakness in the set of his features. Joey put it in his pocket.

'Got to be off now, May,' he said. He laid an envelope on the arm of his chair. 'There's a bit of money there, and my phone number. Any trouble, get in touch. All right?'

'You're a good man, Joey,' she said.

He went down the stairs and into the street. Outside Adgie was admonishing a small boy who had laid an impious hand on the gleaming Jaguar.

'You little bleeder,' he was saying as he assiduously polished the slight mark with a pristine duster, 'ain't you got no respect for private property?'

As Joey approached, the child removed himself to a safe distance.

'Fuck off,' he shouted. 'Next time I see that heap, me an' my mates'll shit all over it.' He scurried round the corner.

'Kids,' said Adgie.

Joey laughed. 'You was one once,' he said.

In the car, as it made its way back to Park Lane, Joey briefed Adgie on an assignment.

'Young Freddie Bates,' he said. 'Did you know him?'

'Not very well,' replied Adgie. 'Knew his old man. He's away, isn't he?'

'That's right. When you drop me I want you to come back

here. Put yourself about a bit. See what you can find out. Young Freddie's dead. Drug overdose. I want names, who he knocked about with, where he got the gear.'

'Right. Will do,' said Adgie.

Joey breezed into the office, where Francesca and Jane were chatting away in Spanish.

'Buenas tardes, senoritas,' he said.

Francesca turned to him with a bland smile.

'Qué tal, hombre?' she said.

'Not so bad, Duchess,' Joey replied. 'Let's go up. Coffee, Jane?'

'Right away, Mr. Bello.'

In the private sitting room Francesca curled herself up on the settee.

'What's the word?' she said.

'Just been to see Freddie's wife. She's in a bit of a state. She can't help much. Seems the kid kept things to himself.'

'So what's the next step? When do we have some action?'

'You're a right little bloodthirsty bastard, aren't you?' said Joey. 'Well, I've sent Adgie down the Dale to do a bit of digging. We'll see what he comes up with. You and me will go up to Islington and have a chat with Ace. Then we'll make up our minds what to do next.'

'You're going to have a pop at the pushers then?'

'You're picking up the jargon a bit sharpish,' said Joey, a note of admiration in his voice.

'Been chatting up Harry, haven't I,' she said. 'Picking up some local colour. I know about the Dale. They wear strides, not trousers. If a geezer is a million, he's a racing certainty, good as gold. One of our'n is a member of the firm. If you're tucked up you've been cheated. A naughty girl doesn't drop her knickers, she whips off her palmers. How'm I doing so far?'

'Very well. Talk like that to your old man and he'll have you up the steps of the Bailey.'

'That pompous old prick. If he's for the prosecution I'm sure to get chucked.'

Joey looked at her quizzically. What makes this young woman tick, he thought. She's not in it for the money. She hasn't drawn a cent out of the firm. Aloud he said, 'There's nothing in this caper cash-wise.'

'Who gives a damn about money? Not me,' she said. 'I've got enough of that commodity. Ask me for anything up to half a million and I'll give it to you. You're opening up a lot of doors for me, Joey, doors that I couldn't open on my tod. So let's have a crusade. Let's sort out the ungodly and smite them hip and thigh. Let's do the only thing that's to be done with life.'

'What's that?' enquired Joey.

'Why, live it. To the full.'

Joey laughed and put his hands together in a round of applause. 'Well said, Duchess. You ought to be in politics.'

'Maybe I will be – one day. In the meantime I'm quite happy as I am. But who knows what the future will bring.'

'We'll tackle the future when we come to it,' said Joey.

'Fair enough. I suppose one day we'll go our separate ways. It'll be a sad day for me.'

'Leave it out,' Joey replied. 'I'll just let Ace know to expect us tonight. You go and get the war-paint on.'

He picked up the telephone.

Joey, Francesca and Ace had their heads together in the latter's private room behind the restaurant. They had dined well. A feature of the meal had been a delicious chateaubriand washed down by a delectable young Beaujolais, served slightly chilled as is the modern fashion in France.

Joey remarked on the superb quality of the meat.

'Courtesy of the Weasel,' said Ace.

'Didn't know that he was in the butchery business,' said Joey.

'He's in everything, so long as it shows a profit,' said Ace. 'He picked up a dozen fillets for me. Prime Aberdeen. I'm reserving them for special clients.'

'We're honoured,' said Francesca.

Ace turned on a dazzling smile.

'My dear Duchess, nothing is too good for you,' he said.

Joey interrupted the exchange of compliments. 'Let's get down to business,' he said.

'I'm all ears,' said Ace. 'What's the programme?'

Joey briefly recounted the story of his visit to Parkhurst and the subsequent meeting with May Bates.

'That's the position. I owe Freddie Bates, so I've got to do something. You know what'll happen if I don't.'

'Freddie'll go over the wall and try to do something about it on his tod,' said Ace. 'He'll be on a hiding to nothing. He'll end up either in a wood overcoat or with another fifteen added on to what he's doing now.'

'Correct. That's the position.'

'Understood, Joey. So what do you propose?'

'Simply this. I'm going to claim the bastard responsible and then make sure that Freddie knows the result. I'll need your help.'

'It's there. Goes without saying,' said Ace.

'Right. I've started by putting Adgie on to it. He's come up with a name.'

'Which is . . .?' queried Ace.

'Roscoe.'

'I know the geezer. Works from Lancaster Gate tube station. His minder is Billy Crowe. That the one?'

'That's him. Little guy with a beard and long hair. Now here's the plan. I want to snatch him and put the frighteners on. Adgie's organising the wheels. We go to work tomorrow night. You and me in the la-di . . .'

'La-di? What's that?' said Francesca.

'La-di-da. Car.'

Joey went on. 'We have him away round the corner. Adgie's doing the driving. I give him a bit of treatment. He's got no class, he'll cough the lot. We truss him up like a turkey and drop him off in front of the nick at Paddington. Pin a little note on him. Pusher ready for nicking or something like that. He'll have plenty of evidence on him.'

'That'll put the cat among the pigeons,' said Ace.

'Exactly,' said Joey. 'That's what I want. They'll get the message higher up. It won't scare 'em. Just show that somebody's after 'em.'

'Good psychology,' said Francesca. 'Where do I come in?'

'Later, Duchess, later. There'll be plenty for you to do.'

'Hope so,' she said. 'I get bored when there's no action.'

The nondescript Ford parked up on the one-way system at Lancaster Gate attracted no attention. To outward appearances the little man behind the wheel was a mini-cab driver. The spade sitting beside him, engaged in an animated conversation with the white man in the rear seat, was probably planning a tour of the Bayswater night-spots. From his position in the driving seat Adgie had a clear view of the pavement in front of the station.

Every precaution had been taken to avoid any possibility of identification. That morning Adgie had purchased the Ford from a back street dealer in Fulham. It was a cash transaction. With the aid of a few spare parts and his nimble fingers, Adgie had transformed a wreck into a runner. When the job was over the car would be abandoned some distance away from the scene of the crime. There it would collect its plethora of parking tickets and would be finally treated as a derelict vehicle and towed away by the local council.

'Heads up,' said Adgie. 'There's Billy Crowe.'

It was indeed the minder, a large man with a pronounced beer-gut, who emerged from the station and looked around him. Apparently satisfied that the coast was clear, he turned towards the entrance to the station and made a beckoning motion. The response was immediate. A little man wearing a long raincoat, bearded and with long hair drooping over the collar of his garment, came out of the station and took his stance on the forecourt. Roscoe was ready for trading.

'Right, Adgie,' said Joey. 'Go!'

The Ford roared up to within a couple of yards of the unsuspecting Roscoe, Joey launched himself from the rear seat, shot a vicious right hook into Crowe's beer-gut and laid hands on his quarry. Crowe collapsed like a punctured balloon, Joey threw Roscoe bodily into the rear seat of the car, climbed in beside him and the car shot off round the corner.

For Adgie it was a cake-walk. He weaved his way through the traffic, got into Sussex Gardens to the accompaniment of some hooting of horns from the drivers he'd carved up on the way, and finally brought the Ford to a halt in a deserted side street near St. Mary's hospital. He remained in the driving seat. Joey dragged the terrified Roscoe onto the pavement, where he was joined by Ace.

Joey slammed his victim against the adjacent wall.

'Keep fucking quiet,' he said, his voice low and menacing. It was an unnecessary warning. Roscoe had no breath left. He had even less after Joey had belted him twice in the guts.

They were three men standing in a confidential group in a quiet street. The smallest of the three was breathing heavily. He had probably had too much to drink and his friends were caring for him. At least that's how it would have seemed to a casual passer-by.

Joey placed his face close to Roscoe's ear. 'Right, you fucking whoreson. Cough,' he said.

Roscoe was regaining his breath and also some of his courage.

'What's the fucking game?' he said.

'Who's your guv'nor? Where do you get your fucking gear. If you don't cough – now – my mate will cut your fucking balls off.'

Ace produced a blade. He let Roscoe have a sight of it before seizing his testicles none too gently. Roscoe opened his mouth to howl. Joey filled the aperture with a bunch of knuckles, knocking Roscoe's front teeth into his tonsils. His voice became an animal growl.

'Cough, you cunting toe-rag. Cough.'

Ace ripped away the front of Roscoe's trousers with the point of the knife and laid the cold steel against the wet penis.

Roscoe had already lost control of his bladder. A bubbling cry came from his throat.

'No . . . no . . . don't . . .'

Joey removed the hand covering the terrified man's mouth.

'Talk,' he said.

'Brandon. Wholesale textiles. Broadley Street, off Edgware Road.'

Ace's voice came through, calm, soft, but somehow terrifying. 'Shall I cut him?'

'Leave it. Wrap him up,' said Joey.

Ace dived into the back of the car and produced the rolls of adhesive tape which were lying in readiness on the back seat. Within the space of half a minute the luckless Roscoe was trussed up like a turkey, manhandled into the car and the abductors were on their way, Adgie driving well within the limit and with due care and attention.

The Ford made its way along Praed Street and swung left at the Edgware Road.

'Slow up at Paddington nick,' said Joey. Adgie nodded and, once over the crossing at Harrow Road, touched the brake pedal. Joey threw Roscoe onto the pavement while the car was still moving, Adgie dropped a gear as Joey pulled the door closed and the Ford sped off in the direction of Maida Vale.

A surprised pedestrian regarded the writhing form and bent down to read the writing on the scrap of paper pinned to the bound man's coat. 'One pusher ready for nicking,' he murmured. He marched into the police station to report his strange find.

Adgie dropped Joey and Ace at the rear of the Cumberland.

'Lose the motor, Adgie. See you at the office in the morning,' said Joey.

As the two men strolled across Marble Arch toward Park Lane, Ace voiced a doubt.

'Reckon he was telling the truth?' he said.

'I'll soon find out,' replied Joey. 'I'll put a check on this chap Brandon first thing tomorrow. See what turns up.'

'Nothing else for the time being?'

'Not just now. I'll be in touch,' said Joey.

Marion brought him the report on Brandon at eleven o'clock the following morning, and Joey scanned the single page of typescript. On the surface the man appeared to be perfectly respectable, a wholesaler of textiles in a fairly substantial way, creditworthy and with an unblemished business record. His home was a flat in Portland Place for which he had paid two hundred thousand pounds three years ago. He was unmarried, and there was no mention of any romantic attachment. Joey's eye was caught by a single sentence at the bottom of the sheet. 'Has personal connections in Marbella, southern Spain'.

Clipped to the report was an agency photograph of a group taken at Ascot. Joey turned the photograph over and read the caption on the back. 'Mr. Henry Brandon (centre) with friends' it said. So, the fellow was in the social swim, said Joey to himself. He looked at the photograph closely and saw a middle-aged man slightly above medium height with a square, determined face and a somewhat prominent nose. He had a trim figure inside the Ascot regalia, and altogether gave the impression of a man who knew his way about.

He was re-reading the report when the internal telephone rang.

'Detective Chief Superintendent Duval, sir. Speaking from a public phone,' said Marion.

'Put him through,' said Joey.

There was a click and Duval came on the line. He spoke without preamble.

'Can we have a meeting, Joey?' he said.

'When and where?'

'Say the Cumberland. In half an hour.'

'I'll be there,' said Joey.

He replaced the receiver. He had a good idea what Duval

wanted to talk about. By now a report on the finding of a drug-pusher, bound and gagged and with his pockets filled with heroin and cocaine, would have found its way into the office of the head of the Serious Crimes Squad. Right, thought Joey, we'll see what our policeman friend has to say. He donned the lightweight jacket which was draped over the back of his chair and made his way down the stairs. He pushed open the door of the front office.

'Just going over to the Cumberland, Marion,' he said. 'Back in fifteen minutes.'

Outside, Adgie was polishing an invisible blemish on the Jag.

'OK, Adgie,' said Joey. The little man nodded.

'Lose the car all right?'

An impish grin appeared on Adgie's face.

'Yeah. Left it on Constitution Hill, outside the Palace. The Bomb Squad'll be crawling all over it by now.'

Joey laughed. 'Wicked little bleeder,' he said. 'See you later.'

He strolled round Marble Arch and entered the Cumberland by a rear door. Duval was already waiting in the lounge. Joey pulled up a chair and sat down.

'What's on your mind, John?' he said.

'A little matter of a known drug-pusher found on the pavement outside Paddington nick,' said Duval. 'All strapped up with tape. Pockets filled with dope. What do you know about it?'

'Why should I know anything about it?' countered Joey.

'Come off it, Joey. You went down to see Freddie Bates in Parkhurst the other day. Then you paid his wife a visit. Young Freddie died recently. Overdose of heroin. Two plus two equals four.'

'So if I did something about it I've done your lot a favour.'

'You should leave it to us, Joey. The Drug Squad has already got Operation Vulture going on in your manor. Doesn't do us any favours when somebody jumps the gun. Puts people on their guard.'

'Operation Vulture? What's that?'

'A big drug bust. I don't need to tell you to keep it under your hat. It's coming off any day now.'

'Nothing to do with me,' said Joey. 'I'm not into the drug scene. Anyway, what will they do? Nick a bunch of cowboys and stick them away for a few years? The big fellers carry on, business as usual.'

'We'll have them too. All in good time.'

'Arseholes, John. The top men have too much protection. Maybe Maggie should privatise the Drug Squad. What's her battle cry? Make 'em leaner and more active.'

Remembering some of the beer-bellies on members of the CID, Duval was unable to restrain a laugh.

'You've got a point there, Joey. Don't labour it. Anyway, what are you up to?'

'It's a personal matter, John. Like, I owe somebody. Let's leave it at that.'

'Can't do anything else, can I? Just be careful, Joey, that's all. If I have to nick you, I will. It wouldn't give me any pleasure, but that's the way things go.'

'I'll remember that, John. Thanks. Anything else you want to get off your chest?'

'No. Oh, by the way, how's that attractive partner of yours?'

'The Duchess? She's fine.'

'I'd like to meet her some day.'

'You will, John. You will.'

Joey rose to his feet. 'I'll leave by the back,' he said. 'See you.'

The burly man came out from behind his newspaper and followed Joey towards the back of the lounge. He emerged into the street and looked both ways. His quarry had vanished. Then came a tap on his shoulder. He turned and came face to face with the man he was supposed to follow.

'All right, mate, what's the game?' said Joey.

'Don't know what you're talking about.'

'You've been following me. I don't like it.'

'So what,' said the burly man truculently.

'You'd better give me a good reason, or I'll kick your arse from here to Marble Arch.'

The man reached into an inside pocket and drew out a small leather wallet which he flipped open.

'Detective Sergeant Crowther, CID,' he said. 'I'm acting under instructions.'

'Well, I'm giving you some instructions, you stupid prick. Piss off. If I see your silly face again I'll alter it so your own mother won't know you. And tell your guv'nor to send somebody more intelligent next time. Got it?'

Detective Inspector Crowther knew when he was licked. He turned and plodded away. He did not relish the prospect of the coming interview with Commander Finch, when he would have to report that his cover had been blown.

Ace Johnson was indeed a womaniser. It was no secret to his close friends, though he conducted his numerous affairs discreetly. On one occasion, after they had both had a good drink, Joey had brought the matter up.

'Beats me why you bother with chasing birds,' he said. 'You've got a lovely wife indoors and a fine couple of kids. Isn't that enough?'

With the gravity of the slightly inebriated, Ace replied in his usual colourful language.

'Belle. I worship her. Couldn't live without her. I'd crawl over broken glass to eat her shit. But I've got to tell you the truth, Joey. She's bloody hopeless in bed. I give her one now and then. She lies on her back, doesn't move. One time she was eating chocolates while I was banging away. When I've shot my load she gives me a kiss, says it was very nice, rolls over and goes to sleep.'

Joey nodded. 'See what you mean, Ace. It's a pity. Lovely woman going to waste.'

Ace warmed to his subject, the bit between his teeth.

'I've got a big, beautiful beast in my trousers, Joey. It needs exercise. Black or white, the chicks go mad about it.

They'll play with it, suck it, take it any way I want to give it, underneath, on top, front or back. They get their pleasure, I get mine.'

Once more Joey nodded his agreement.

'I'm not taking anything away from Belle,' Ace went on dreamily. 'I give her everything she wants, clothes, jewellery, a nice place to live. She's quite happy taking care of the kids.' He paused. 'I'll never leave her. One day I won't be able to get it up any more. Come that day the kids'll be grown up and I'll settle for happy families. Whatever happens me and Belle will always be together.'

'Leave it out, Ace,' said Joey. 'Hearts and fucking flowers. You'll have me in tears in a minute.'

The subject was never brought up again, but whenever Joey saw Ace and Belle together he had a slight lump in his throat.

It was a fine, sunny afternoon and Ace was pursuing his latest conquest. Her name was Sandra, she came from Trinidad and Ace had met her the previous evening in a small night spot frequented mainly by West Indian musicians.

She had been called up to the stand to do a number. She accompanied herself on the piano and her voice was thin, clear and pure, perfectly matched to the old standard she was working. Coming to the reprise, she fixed her eyes on Ace. Her fingers rested lightly on the piano keys as she softly vamped a musical background to the words. She sang directly at him and there was no mistaking the message in her eyes nor the meaning with which she charged the words of the lyric, which were in themselves emotional enough. It was as though she were saying 'Mister Ace, I am going to use you, and that right soon'.

It was showing out with a vengeance and the audience, mainly men, recognised it. Though they knew that the singer didn't give a monkey's about applause, they nevertheless put their hands together. As for Ace, he was captivated. She was small with a slight figure and not particularly beautiful, but her voice did everything for her. She came down from the stand and joined him for a drink.

'Did you like my music, mister Ace?'

'I loved it. I'd like to hear more.'

'I have a piano at my place. I shall be home tomorrow afternoon. Here's my card.'

It had been as simple as that. Now Ace, impeccably garbed in what he referred to as his carnival outfit, gaily coloured shirt, white linen trousers and white shoes, was ringing the bell at a small house in Hamilton Terrace.

The maid who opened the door evidently expected the visitor.

'Miss Sandra is in the lounge, sir,' she said. 'Would you go through?'

Ace went through. Sandra was indeed waiting in the lounge, a large and finely furnished room deeply carpeted in white with white leather settees and easy chairs. The principal feature was a Steinway grand piano. Sandra was wearing a white house-coat which provided a startling contrast to her dusky skin. Ace suspected that the housecoat was her only garment.

She took both his hands in hers.

'Welcome to my humble abode, mister Ace,' she said. 'What would you like to drink?'

Ace looked at her glass, which she had set down on an occasional table. It contained some sort of milky fluid.

'What are you drinking?' he said.

'Pastis. The real stuff. Home made and guaranteed to blow your mind. Like some?'

'If it's good enough for you, it's good enough for me.'

As she poured from a plain bottle and added ice and water, Ace was enchanted. I've got a real little raver here, he thought. I'm going to enjoy it.

She handed him the drink and moved over to seat herself at the piano.

'Would you like to hear my version of "La Vie en Rose," mister Ace?'

'Yes please.'

She struck a few opening chords, then launched into the plaintive number made famous by Edith Piaf. She sang in the original French with a faint West Indian accent. She came to the end, rose from her seat, took a drink from her glass and came over to Ace, standing directly in front of him.

'I like to sing that song before I make love,' she said. She unfastened the belt of her housecoat and opened it wide. As Ace had guessed, she wore nothing beneath it. Her breasts, though small, were perfectly formed, the stomach flat and the hips and legs firm and nicely rounded. He reached for her, but she evaded his grasp.

'Not just yet, mister Ace,' she said. 'Lie back and relax. I'm gonna pleasure you as you've never been pleasured before.'

She knelt down as Ace leaned back in the settee. Quickly she undid his belt, operated the zip on his trousers and drew them down, repeating the action with his pants.

'It's . . . beautiful,' she gasped, staring at Ace's considerable erection. She closed her lips gently round the head and slowly engulfed the stem almost to its whole length. Ace half-closed his eyes and gave himself up to the sensation. She began to move her head backwards and forwards slowly and rhythmically. Ace's hands reached automatically for her shoulders, but she shrugged them off as she stepped up the tempo. Ace groaned as the hot flood of semen flowed from him.

'You liked that, mister Ace?'

Ace's voice was a trifle shaky, but he managed a gallant reply.

'An understatement, dear lady. I loved it.'

'Now you just take off your clothes,' she said, 'and lie right down on that white rug over there. Momma is gonna bring this little soldier to attention again.'

As Ace stretched himself out on the soft rug she was on him like a tigress. As Ace reacted she hoisted herself and, parting her legs, lowered herself onto him. As she came down, she wriggled her hips and groaned as she accommodated herself to absorbing his entire length into her.

They passed an hour in ceaseless congress, during which time they explored every possible position known to those skilled in the art of copulation. Ace came again and again. Finally, exhausted, they lay side by side, breathing heavily. She was the first to recover. As she rolled over preparatory to getting to her feet, the sleeve of her housecoat fell back, and Ace caught a glimpse of the needle scars on the inside of her forearm. Jesus, he thought, I've hooked a mainliner. An idea passed through his head. Maybe I can pick up a bit of information.

She sat on the settee and reached out a hand to take a couple of hand-rolled joints from a silver box.

'Do you smoke?' she asked.

'Occasionally.'

'Come and join me.'

He sat beside her on the settee and they lit up. Ace drew in the fumes. First class gear, he thought, Acapulco Gold or I'm a Dutchman. This chick must have good connections. He was conscious of the small warm palm caressing his pubes.

'You certainly are a wonderful screw, mister Ace,' she said.

'May I say you're not so bad yourself.'

'I could get very fond of you,' she said dreamily.

'Hold on, baby. No strings . . .'

'I don't want them either. If we could do it now and then . . .'

'Suits me,' said Ace.

They sat for a while in silence savouring the fragrant weed. Her caressing hand was still active and he felt a stirring in his loins. He shot a sudden question at her.

'How did you get on smack?'

She looked at him questioningly. He reached across, pulled back the sleeve of her housecoat.

'Careless of me,' she said.

'So, how come?'

'About a year ago. I lost my voice. Went to specialists, tried everything. No dice. Somebody suggested heroin, said it would relax me. I tried it and it worked. Simple as that.'

'Is it good gear? Who's your supplier?' Ace's tone was quiet and non-committal.

'You're not on it?'

'No, but I've got friends who are. Like to do them a favour.'

'All right. His name's Brandon. He's my agent. He also owns this house. He's a top man, very well connected. He has a house in Geneva where his wife and two daughters live, another place in Jersey and a villa in Marbella.'

'Are you screwing him?'

'No. He's got a dick like a withered prawn. I tried him once. It was a fucking fiasco.'

Ace was delighted. What a coincidence, he thought, a nugget of priceless information falling into his hands so easily.

'I'll give you a telephone number and a password,' she went on. 'Don't flash it around.' Her hand gripped him tightly. 'I hope you won't flash this little number around too much either,' she said. She ground out the joint in the ashtray and brought two hands to bear on him. He was hard as a rock.

'Let's play some more games,' she said. She bent over him, ready, lips parted to start again at the beginning.

Later that evening Ace joined Joey at the house in Park Lane.

'Guess what I've got!' he said.

'The clap?' said Joey.

Ace laughed. 'That'll be the day. No, man. What I've got is the full SP on Brandon.'

Ace went on to describe the events of the afternoon, and ended by handing Joey a scrap of paper on which was written a telephone number and a single word.

'That's the private number. The password proves that you're kosher.'

'Blimey, Ace, you're a million,' said Joey. 'That's just too good to be true. What a breakthrough! I thought it was going to take us months to get that information.'

'Just one thing,' said Ace. 'There'll be no comeback on the chick?'

'Forget it. From now on I handle the business personally. There'll be no comeback for anybody. That includes me.'

'I'll take your word for it,' said Ace. 'Dunno what you're letting yourself in for. Just watch out. You've heard about the Yardies?'

'Yes,' replied Joey.

'They're handling crack. It's lethal. One dose and you're hooked. They're animals. Stop at nothing, so watch it.'

'Don't worry. I will.'

'I'm off then. See you later.'

'And Ace. Thanks again.'

As soon as Ace had left, Joey picked up the phone. Harry was on duty.

'Give me an outside line, Harry. Don't monitor this call,' he said.

Joey glanced at the scrap of paper and dialled the number. The response was almost immediate.

'Brandon,' said a smooth cultured voice.

'Eureka,' said Joey.

There was a short pause and then, 'Just a moment. I'll take your call on another phone.'

Another phone my arse, thought Joey. He's switching on a recorder.

There was another short pause and the voice came to him again. Now it was altogether more business-like.

'What can I do for you?' said Brandon.

'Business. Can we meet?'

'To whom am I speaking?'

'Names later. When and where?'

Brandon was obviously on the ball and accustomed to dealing with calls out of the blue.

'I shall be free at nine this evening. Perhaps you would call on me.' He gave an address which Joey had no need to commit to memory.

'I'll be there,' said Joey. He hung up.

Precisely at nine o'clock Joey pressed the button of Flat 4 of an imposing block in Portland Place.

'Who is it?' said the voice on the intercom.

'Eureka,' said Joey.

'Come up please. Flat 4 on the second floor.'

A buzzer sounded and the lock on the door was released. Joey passed through into a carpeted foyer and proceeded to the lift which quickly whisked him to the second floor. He pressed the bell at the door of Flat 4, which opened immediately. Brandon stood in the doorway.

'Please come in,' he said. He led the way into a large and luxuriously furnished room where every item from the deep carpet to the pictures on the walls were indicative of the wealth of the owner.

'Would you care for a drink?' said Brandon.

'No thanks,' said Joey. 'I'd like to get down to business.'

'Just as you wish. Please sit down.'

He motioned his visitor towards an easy chair and took a seat himself.

'Now sir,' said Brandon. 'You mentioned a word which satisfies me as to your credentials. Might I now ask to whom I am speaking?'

'You may. The name is Carpenter, Gerald Carpenter. I'll come to the point. I represent a syndicate which is looking for a source of supply of smack. We want pure so that we can cut it. Your name has been given by a mutual friend.'

'Who is . . .?'

'Really, Mr Brandon. You should know better. No doubt he'll tell you himself at some later date. Meanwhile, can you supply?'

'What quantities were you thinking of?'

'We'll take all you can give us.'

Joey could have sworn that Brandon's nostrils twitched.

'You'd like to test a sample?' he said.

'Please.'

Brandon rose to his feet and walked over to where a brightly-coloured painting hung on the wall. Joey would have guessed that it was an original Picasso. He swung the frame back on its hinges to disclose a fairly large wall safe and, taking a bunch of keys from his pocket, inserted one of them in the lock and opened the door. Reaching inside he extracted a plastic sachet, which he brought to a small table at Joey's elbow. Breaking the seal, he shook a small quantity of the white powder onto the glass surface. Joey moistened a finger, took up a few grains and transferred them to his tongue. There was no doubt in his mind. It was first grade pure.

Now the situation changed. Joey got to his feet and confronted his host, but there was no friendliness in his voice. It was vibrant with an awesome menace.

'You fucking whoreson bastard. There's a kid lying in his grave. Son of a friend of mine. It's down to you. You're going to join him.'

Joey delivered a crushing right to the jaw and the man went down, out to the wide. Joey picked up the sachet from the table and, bending over the unconscious body, forced Brandon's jaws open. The contents of the sachet were poured into the open mouth. One hand on the top of Brandon's head and the other beneath his jaw, Joey forced him to swallow.

'Die, you fucking bastard, die,' he growled.

Brandon's body stiffened, then went limp. A ghastly, rasping sound came from the half-open mouth. He was seconds away from death. Joey got up and looked around him. Now he had to find the tape recorder which he had no doubt had been switched on before he entered the room.

It did not take him long to find it. The microphone was concealed in the base of a table lamp and the thin wire led to a drawer in the elegant escritoire on which the lamp stood. Flipping back the cover of the recorder, Joey extracted the tape and put it in his pocket. Now he went to the body on the floor and took the bunch of keys from the trousers.

The safe, once opened, disclosed not only a hoard of drugs but also a large quantity of Treasury notes in neat bundles. Joey stuffed away as many of the bundles as his pockets would hold. He left the flat and descended to the ground floor by way of the service stairs, where a door led to the mews at the rear of the building. He let himself out and strolled away in the direction of Oxford Circus.

The following morning Joey paid a call on May Bates. He carried two press cuttings and a large manilla envelope.

'Go and see Freddie as soon as you can,' he told her. 'Show him these cuttings and tell him the account's been settled.'

He laid the envelope on the table. 'This is for you,' he said. 'Help to keep the wolf from the door.'

May peered inside the envelope and gasped.

'What's this? Blimey, Joey, there must be about twenty grand in here.'

'Something like that,' said Joey. 'Call it the wages of sin.'

8. *Villainy in Spain*

International policing is no simple matter, as any member of Interpol would bear witness. Professional jealousy between the forces of law and order in different countries, matters of protocol and the difficulties of operating the complex procedures under which a criminal may be extradited from the country in which he has sought refuge, are constraints which hamper the proper administration of justice. Concorde can fly the Atlantic in a matter of four hours or so, any country in the world is a telephone call away, the latest technology is at the disposal of law enforcement officers, yet a criminal may remove himself from his native soil and cock a snook at any attempts to bring him back to stand trial for his crimes.

No such constraints interfere with the lines of communication in the world of international crime. The aeroplane and the telephone have abolished national boundaries and there is no law that governs the swift administration of their kind of retribution. A sentence of death may be passed and carried out within twenty-four hours without recourse to a lengthy trial. The executioner need not take the risk of carrying a weapon through Customs. Poison or the knife are his favourite means of despatching his victim to the next world. Unmarked graves all over the world are the final resting place of those who have offended against the code. They had nowhere else to hide.

The expected call from the Costa del Sol came through as Joey was drinking his mid-morning coffee.

'Hiya, Joey. How's it going?' said Micky.

'No complaints. What's on your mind?' said Joey.

'Something's cropped up. Can we have a meet?'

'Sure. I'm coming over to see the Bruno fight. You'll be there?'

'You bet. See you then.'

'See you,' said Joey. He put down the phone.

He had no illusions about the significance of the call. The news of Roscoe's capture and Brandon's death would have reached Spain in double-quick time. Micky, George and Ronnie must now be wondering if Joey had suddenly gone bananas, for there could be little doubt in their minds that, somehow or other, Joey was mixed up in the affair. Now the music had to be faced.

He got through to Marion on the internal phone.

'Get everybody onto this,' he said. 'Five first class seats on a flight to Malaga on Friday, returning Monday. Book five rooms with bath, a decent hotel within easy reach of Marbella, Friday to Monday. Arrange a large self-drive car. Tell Adgie to fix an International driving permit with the AA. Is the Duchess there?'

'She's down in the gym.'

'Ask her to come up and see me. And get me Ace on the phone.'

'Very good, Mr. Bello.'

He was speaking to Ace within seconds.

'Ace? This is important. I'm off to Spain on Friday. See the Bruno fight. I want you and the Weasel with me. All right?'

'No problem. Fill me in on the details later.'

'Will do.'

As Joey hung up Francesca walked in.

'What's on, Joey?' she said.

'We're off to the Costa del Sol on Friday. See a boxing match. Like to come?'

'Try and keep me away. Who's we?'

'Me, Ace, the Weasel and Adgie.'

'The cavalry. All right. I'll make one,' she said.

Joey laughed. 'You certainly are picking up the jargon,' he said.

Duval and Joey sat facing each other in a corner of a small bar in Pimlico. Apart from the two men, the bar was deserted.

'What did you want to see me about?' asked Joey.

Duval's face bore the sad look of a man who had an unpleasant duty to perform and was determined to carry it out.

'I think you know, Joey,' he said.

'Haven't a clue, but carry on.'

'Chap called Brandon. Found dead in his flat. Probable cause of death a large quantity of heroin administered orally. What do you know about it?'

'Not a thing,' said Joey cheerfully. 'Got any evidence? Eye witnesses? Fingerprints?'

'No.'

'There you are then. Typical case of unsolved crime. That is if a crime has been committed.'

'The Drug Squad has had this man under observation . . .'

Joey interrupted quickly. 'Under observation or under protection?'

'All right. Point taken. That makes no difference. It's a possible case of murder which I shall have to investigate.'

'Investigate away, John. You haven't got a cat in hell's chance. A bloke like Brandon must have thousands of enemies. I'll tell you one thing. If I knock anybody off it's for a very good reason.'

Duval nodded. 'You've answered all my questions. Now I'll tell you something. Stop taking the law into your own hands.'

'My turn to say point taken. Let's leave it out, shall we?'

'Suits me.'

'That's it then. By the way, last time we met I had a tail on me. I claimed him outside the back door of the Cumberland. Chap called Crowther.'

'I know him,' said Duval. 'One of Finch's goons. Thick as two short planks. Thanks for the tip.'

'A pleasure,' said Joey. He looked at his watch. 'Got to get along. A bit busy. Off to Spain on Friday to see the Bruno fight. You going?'

'Not me,' said Duval. 'Half the Met will be there anyway.'

'That's a racing certainty,' said Joey. He got up to leave. 'A last word,' he said.

'What's that?'

'If I ever walk up the steps at the Bailey on a charge of murder, I'll know who to blame.'

'Who?'

'Me. For being careless. See you later.'

That afternoon Duval was called to Finch's office. The Commander was in a bad mood.

'What's happening about this chap Bello?' he said.

'Nothing,' said Duval.

'You've been seen with him on two occasions. What were you doing?'

Duval was too old a hand to be caught by that one. 'It's in my reports, sir. I'm sure you've seen them. Pursuing enquiries. Access to suspect's premises denied. No grounds for a search warrant. No grounds for arrest. Interviews took place in the lounge of an hotel. Strictly according to regulations.'

Jesus Christ, thought Finch, this bugger is taking the piss out of me. He lost his temper.

'Your reports tell me fuck-all. I want to see results, Duval. Now get this cunt fitted up. That's an order.'

Duval's bland smile would have rivalled the expression on the face of a Buddha.

'I'm sorry you have to use such intemperate language sir,' he said. 'As to your orders, I'm afraid I must insist that they are confirmed at a higher level – in writing. I shall then be only too pleased to carry them out.'

Finch's eyes narrowed. He had walked into a trap and he knew it. He controlled his rage, but there was a tremor in his voice as he addressed his subordinate.

'There's something going on between you and this villain Bello. I don't know what it is, but by fucking Christ I'll find out. Then I'll fix you if it's the last thing I do.'

'It may well be,' said Duval.

'What?' Finch roared out the word.

'The last thing you do,' said Duval. Without waiting to be dismissed he turned and walked out.

He left behind him a very worried man. Finch knew he was facing a crisis. The Rubber Heels were on his back. So was Matthew Gill. He could expect no help from that quarter, for he was well aware that Gill would not put out a finger to help him. In addition he had raised a suspicion in the mind of a fairly highly-placed colleague. The net was closing in.

The Bello entourage was in high spirits as it disembarked at Malaga airport. On the flight Joey and Francesca had been abstemious and Adgie was on orange juice. Ace and the Weasel, however, were in holiday mood, and the stock of free champagne offered to first-class passengers suffered as a result.

The strangely assorted quintet passed through Customs without incident. Francesca's colloquial Spanish was adequate to meet the occasion and Ace's mildly boisterous behaviour raised no more than a smile from the amused official. On the other side of Customs a polite young man emerged from the crowd and came up to Joey.

'Mr Bello?'

'That's right.'

'Your car is on the front, sir. I hope it will be large enough for your party.'

It was the latest Citroen with room and to spare for the five of them. Adgie gave the vehicle a comprehensive once-over.

'My driver,' explained Joey to the attentive young man, who turned to Adgie.

'You are – er – accustomed to driving in Spain?'

Adgie gave the man a withering glance.

'If I 'ad a quid for every mile I've drove on the Continong I'd be a bleeding millionaire,' he said.

The young man managed a weak smile and handed over the keys.

'If you would be good enough to leave the car on the park

here on Monday, we'll see to collection,' he said. 'You may leave the keys in the glove box.'

Joey signed the forms and slipped the young man a 'green', the thousand peseta note worth about five pounds sterling.

'Very good service,' he said. 'Have a drink.'

That Adgie had driven before on what he called the 'wrong side of the road' was apparent. He swung confidently onto the main drag which led to Marbella and in forty minutes came to the fork where the road branched right for Puerto Banus. There he consulted a map, and twenty minutes later turned into the approach to their hotel, a brand new construction overlooking the harbour.

Their accommodation turned out to be five one-bedroom suites, each with its balcony and a view over the Mediterranean.

'Somebody must have pulled a few strings,' commented Francesca.

'Jane,' said Joey. 'Got a boy-friend at the Spanish consulate.'

They settled in and then foregathered in Joey's suite for a discussion on plans for the immediate future.

'First thing is we go along to the fight tomorrow night, just like the others,' he said. 'For the time being I'm playing it by ear. I'll know more about things after the fight. We'll make plans then. All right?'

'We're right with you,' said Ace. The other three nodded agreement.

'Good. From now on we stick together and be prepared for anything that might happen.'

There was a knock on the door and two waiters came in with a large trolley bearing drinks and a plentiful supply of the pre-dinner snacks which the Spanish call tapas: giant prawns, mussels on the half-shell, calamares redolent of garlic and a plethora of other delicacies. Ace, the professional, tasted and approved.

'Somebody in the kitchen knows what he's about,' he said.

The team sat down to dinner shortly after nine o'clock. The food was delicious, the service impeccable.

'This is a great place,' said the Weasel through a mouthful of steak tartare.

'I told the head waiter that Ace was a great friend of Egon Ronay,' said Joey.

'As a matter of fact I am,' said Ace.

'There you are, then,' said Joey. 'Sometimes it pays to tell the truth.'

'The truth is that you slipped him a few greens,' said Francesca.

'That too, Duchess,' replied Joey. They all laughed.

Adgie had ordered fried fish and chips. He regarded the Spanish version of the dish with some distaste.

'They do better'n this at Fishy Fred's down the Dale,' he said.

The following morning the clouds that had begun to gather in the east rolled over Puerto Banus. As the five of them sat down to lunch, the skies opened and the rain came down in sheets. Later, as they sat in the lounge over coffee, the head waiter brought the news that the fight had been postponed owing to the fact that the venue, the Plaza de Toros in Puerto Banus, had been flooded.

'Ah, well,' said Joey philosophically. 'That's it then.'

'Mañana,' said the head waiter helpfully.

'Everything in Spain happens tomorrow,' said Francesca.

Sunday was bright and clear. The sun shone from a cloudless sky and the friendly head waiter was sanguine about the prospect of the fight taking place that evening.

'They work all night, all today,' he said. 'You go. Will be OK.'

'Hope you're right,' said Joey.

They spent the day around the pool. The head waiter was in constant attendance, as though he had taken personal responsibility for the failure of the Spanish weather to come up to scratch. He arranged an alfresco lunch which was a marvel of its kind and would have been more than adequate for twice their number.

Without a trace of self-consciousness, Francesca stripped down to her briefs and stretched out on a sun-lounger.

'This is the life,' she said to Joey, who had just emerged dripping from the pool.

'Don't get too comfortable,' replied Joey. 'I reckon the fun and games won't start until tomorrow, but you never know.'

'When it comes, I'll be ready,' she replied.

The afternoon passed pleasantly, the group at the pool-side exchanging snatches of conversation as they sipped iced tea. It was all very quiet and peaceful. Adgie wandered off in the direction of the garage where he had parked the Citroen. He was obviously not entirely satisfied with the performance of this foreign product, and he soon had his head buried under the bonnet, from where an occasional muttered obscenity gave evidence of his opinion of this load of French rubbish in comparison with his beloved Jaguar.

Ace was engaged in low-voiced conversation with the Weasel as they sat under a large umbrella which protected them from the burning rays of the sun. As he had jocularly remarked earlier in the day, Ace had no desire to add to his permanent tan. 'Man, I only go purple,' he had said. As for the Weasel, he had no use for basking in the sun, maintaining that he was white and intended to stay that way.

At six o'clock Joey proposed a move.

'Better get changed,' he said. 'We'll leave about half-seven. That gives us plenty of time to get down to the bullring.'

They drifted off to their respective quarters to dress for the occasion. When they assembled later in the lounge, it was to find a resplendent Ace awaiting them. He was wearing a dazzling white suit and his gaily-coloured shirt was open almost to the waist to display a large gold medallion. White buckskin shoes and a white Panama hat with a narrow black band completed the ensemble.

'Blimey,' said Adgie, a note of admiration in his voice, 'you don't 'arf make the rest of us look shabby.'

Joey's only comment was to the effect that Ace would make a splendid target if somebody decided to take a pot-shot at them.

'Everybody has to die sometime,' said Ace philosophically. 'I would like to think that I'm suitably attired when I present myself at the Pearly Gates.'

'Even God would be jealous of you in that outfit,' said Francesca irreverently. She herself was dressed in a skin-tight black creation relieved only by the single rope of pearls round her neck. Joey and the Weasel both wore the formal white dinner-jacket and black trousers which were *de rigueur* on the Costa. Adgie was, as usual, clad in his dark blue uniform suit. He led the way to the Citroen, which had taken on an added sheen since its collection at the airport.

'Didn't need all that spit and polish,' said Joey. 'It's only a hire car.'

Adgie's reply was short and to the point.

'Any car I drive 'as to be a car, not a shit-'eap.'

There was no answer to that.

The Plaza de Toros was crowded to capacity. Adgie dropped the team at the entrance and drove off to park the car. As they made their way to their reserved seats, they were able to look down on the sea of figures extending to the edges of the boxing ring. There was a large British contingent and Joey pointed out to Francesca several Old Bill mingling with the spectators, looking anything but official in shirt-sleeve order.

'Be a bad look-out if there's a crime wave in the smoke,' he said. 'The Met will be very short of officers.'

'The Met is always short of officers,' was Francesca's cryptic reply.

From his point of vantage, where he could see without being seen, Joey spent some time surveying the motley throng. He identified many faces familiar to him from the days of Parkhurst and Dartmoor and came to the conclusion that villainy had become a very profitable occupation for a considerable number of his former associates. From what he could see they appeared to be well-dressed and well-provided for even a short holiday in a resort which was accustomed to catering for millionaires.

'See anyone you know?' said Francesca.

'Quite a few, Duchess. If it came to a head-count, I reckon the British villains would outnumber the law by about five to one.'

'Any sign of the opposition?'

'Can't see 'em. Probably the other side of the ring. Don't worry. They'll be about.'

'Who are we looking for?' said Ace.

His reply was interrupted by the sudden appearance of Adgie, who popped up out of nowhere.

'Hello. Where've you been?' said Joey.

'Just looking round. Saw some of the geezers from the Dale. They're 'ere mob-handed.'

Further conversation was made impossible as the amplified voice of the announcer echoed round the bullring. Joey and his companions settled into their seats as the supporting bouts to the main event of the evening came and went. The spectators gave them a lukewarm reception. There was no doubt as to what they were waiting for.

In the event, Lloyd Honeyghan wasted no time in disposing of a certain Gene Hatcher from the United States of America, whose main disability as a contender for the Welterweight Championship of the World lay in being unable to avoid Honeyghan's lethal right hand. The other main event, the heavyweight contest between Britain's Frank Bruno and Reggie Gross, took longer to decide. The American was outclassed from the opening round, but stubbornly refused to go down and stay down. Joey stole a look at Francesca as she leaned forward in her seat, teeth bared and a savage look on her face as Bruno ripped punches into his opponent. She was enjoying the spectacle.

The end came before the expiry of the scheduled ten rounds. Gross was reeling on the ropes as Bruno used him as a punchbag, and there were shouts from the ringside calling for the fight to be stopped. As the referee raised his hands to signal that Gross was no longer in a position to defend himself, a figure launched itself into the ring, shouting at the referee. 'You're a bloody disgrace,' was the cry, which was taken up by several of the spectators at the ringside.

'Who's that fellow?' asked Francesca.

'Bruno's manager, Lawless,' replied Joey.

'Bloody spoilsport,' said Francesca.

The spectators began to drift away when the bout ended.

'Keep close together,' said Joey as his party strolled to the car park. 'Don't think there'll be any bother. Just be careful.'

Adgie had left the Citroen in a position which rendered egress from the park an easy matter.

'What happens now?' asked Francesca.

'People will be going off to parties, Duchess. Down to Silks or the bars in Marbella.'

'What about us?'

'I think we're better off going back to the hotel. I've laid on a late meal. That all right with everybody?'

The others replied in the affirmative. Adgie piloted them swiftly and safely back to the hotel through the crowded streets where the bars were being inundated by the celebrators of the British victory. The head waiter at the hotel led them to a secluded corner of the dining room, where a delicious meal was served. Over coffee Joey put his team in the picture.

'Couldn't say much until I'd been to the fight,' he began. 'I didn't know which way the cat was going to jump. Now I know what to do. Put it in a nutshell, I've got to front some people who won't be very friendly. I'm going to the villa where one of them lives tomorrow morning. I reckon they'll have a welcoming committee for me. This is what I want you to do.'

Clearly and in detail he spelled out what would be required of them. They listened attentively.

'Any questions?' he asked.

Ace spoke for all of them.

'No questions,' he said.

The team checked out the following morning. Their luggage was stowed away in the boot of the Citroen, Adgie was at the wheel with Francesca at his side. Ace and the Weasel occupied the rear seats. Before he entered the taxi which was standing at the hotel entrance, Joey had a brief word with Adgie.

'Follow the taxi. Don't get too close. Watch where I get out. You know what to do after that.'

Adgie nodded. Joey climbed into the taxi and gave directions to the driver. He was under no illusions about the reception which would be waiting for him at his destination. He was equally certain that the precautions he had taken were adequate to meet the situation. As the adrenalin began to flow, he leaned back in his seat and relaxed.

The distance from the hotel to Micky's villa was covered in a matter of ten minutes. At the gate, Joey paid off the driver and stood for a moment as the taxi drove away. He turned and walked resolutely through the gate and into the short drive.

He had guessed correctly that the reception committee would be gathered at the bar adjacent to the swimming pool. As he mounted the few steps that led to the pool area, he saw them, Micky, George and Ronnie, standing close together, drinks in their hands. Nearby, sitting at one of the tables, were two men whom Joey did not recognise, but who bore all the hallmarks of professional heavies.

Ronnie and George had their backs to Joey as he walked briskly along the side of the pool. Micky was the first to see him. As he muttered a few words to his companions they turned as one man.

Micky was the first to speak. There was no friendliness in his voice.

'What's this game you're playing, Bello?' he said.

'Dunno what you're talking about,' said Joey. 'You wanted a meet. Here I am.'

'Don't come the fucking acid with me,' said Micky. 'I'm talking about Roscoe and Brandon. What are you up to?'

Joey looked steadily at his interrogator. His experience told him that Micky was not interested in answers. Whatever he said would only serve to fuel the flames of his anger. Nevertheless he decided to have a go.

'It's a personal matter. There was an account to be settled. I settled it.'

Ronnie, who had a reputation for being mouthy, put his spoke in.

'What the fuck are you talking about? You've put the kybosh on our British operation. You come here yapping about a personal matter. Have you lost your marbles?'

Micky broke in. He jerked his thumb expressively over his shoulder.

'We've got graves up in those hills. One of them's reserved for you.'

That was when it came on top. During the brief conversation the three men had closed in on Joey. Now George swung a vicious right to Joey's head, which Joey tried to avoid, only to run into Ronnie's fist, which impacted on the side of his head. He dropped to one knee as Micky moved to take a hand in the game.

Joey came to his feet. On the way he shot his fist into George's crotch and felt the soft squelch as he connected with his testicles. Micky, in his haste to play his part in the battle, stumbled over Joey's outstretched leg and was off balance for a second. A steel-shod foot driven into his ribs robbed him of breath. With two of his opponents incapacitated for the moment, Joey turned his attention to Ronnie, who had backed away a couple of steps. He had been a hard man in his day, but the months of soft living had eroded his muscles and slowed up his reflexes. He was no match for a superbly fit Joey. He felt a moment of panic as Joey drove a rapid series of punches into his ribs and, as he reeled back from the attack, he lost his footing on the edge of the pool and went arse over tit into the water.

The two heavies had been slow to react to the sudden development in the battle. Now they rose to their feet and advanced menacingly on Joey, one waving an iron bar, the other gripping a chopper. It was precisely then that Joey's reinforcements arrived. Francesca led the way, fists tightly clenched on brass knuckles, her steel-shod feet tapping on the paving round the pool. Behind her, waving pick-axe handles, came Ace and the Weasel. Francesca was emitting a high-pitched scream as she ran towards the mêlée. Disconcerted, the heavies halted in their tracks. The hesitation was their downfall. The brass knuckles flashed, the prancing Francesca launched hand and foot attacks from all angles and Ace and the Weasel swung their weapons at heads and limbs. The heavies went down like ninepins.

Ronnie had meanwhile dragged himself from the pool. The first thing he saw was Francesca's slim back. Under the impression that he was attacking the weakest member of the invading team, he came up behind her and laid his hands on her shoulders. It was a fatal error. She bent her knees, threw him over her head and, as he struggled to regain his feet, she lashed her right foot into his throat. With a tigerish snarl, she hurled herself at him, the brass knuckles beating a tattoo on his ribs. As the bones cracked, he hit the water once more.

Francesca, carried on by the impetus of her attack, went in after him.

In the meantime Joey had concentrated on beating Micky and George into a pulp. It was no contest. Whatever prowess his adversaries had shown in the past, they were now proved to be over the hill. As Francesca climbed out of the pool, appearing to be almost naked, her wet clothing clinging to her body and outlining every curve, Joey looked around him at the inert bodies of his enemies. A few bubbles rising to the surface of the pool were the only evidence of Ronnie's retirement from the conflict.

'Right. On your toes,' yelled Joey. As they ran to the car, Francesca emitted a blood-curdling Indian war cry. Joey gave her a sidelong glance. Christ, he thought, the bloodthirsty little sod is enjoying it.

Adgie was waiting in the Citroen, the engine running. He needed no instructions. As they tumbled into their seats he slammed in the gear lever and within minutes they were on the main drag leading to the airport.

The setback came when they arrived at Malaga. There had been vague rumours that a strike of airport personnel was on the cards when they left the hotel. The rumours turned out to be fact. All outgoing flights were cancelled until further notice.

Francesca had just returned from the ladies' loo, where she had changed into dry clothing. Joey gave her the news.

'We'll have to wait then,' she said.

'Can't do that,' replied Joey. 'The other lot have an army on the coast. There'll be people looking for us before long. We haven't got much time.'

It was Adgie who came up with the solution to the problem.

'What about driving up to the French border?' he said. 'We could make Alicante by tonight. Stay there, make an early start tomorrow. Up the coast road, Valencia, Barcelona. Cross the border at La Junquera. They don't pay no attention there. Just wave you on. We could be in Perpignan before dark.'

'That's an idea,' said Joey. 'What about it?'

'It would be a bit of a lark,' said Francesca. 'I'm for it.'

'Me too,' said Ace.

'Anything for a change,' said the Weasel.

'Right. Let's hit the road,' said Joey.

As they sped along the highway from the airport, Joey kept a close eye on the road behind them. He did not underestimate the opposition. Micky and his associates were powerful and influential figures on the Costa del Sol and numbered on their payroll a horde of spies and informers. Some minor officials were not above accepting favours in cash or in kind. Joey was quite sure that the hunt would be on. He turned to Adgie at his side.

'Put your foot down. We want to get clear of Malaga as quick as we can,' he said.

Francesca, sitting between Ace and the Weasel in the rear of the car, asked the pertinent question.

'You think they'll be after us?'

'It's anybody's guess,' said Joey. 'There'll be people at the airport now, looking for us. They'll know we couldn't fly out. I reckon they'll spend a bit of time searching the area before they tumble that we've scarpered. Let's hope they think we've legged it to Gibraltar.'

'We certainly did some damage back there,' said Ace.

The Weasel laughed. 'Did you see the way those two goons performed! They didn't know what had hit them.'

'What happened to Ronnie, Duchess?' asked Joey.

'Ronnie?'

'The geezer you took for a swim.'

'Oh, him. He's probably a goner. I drop-kicked him in the throat and smashed his ribs. He was still underwater when we had it away.'

'Jesus,' said Joey. 'That's put the cat among the pigeons.'

Francesca cocked an eyebrow. 'Wasn't that the object of the exercise?'

Adgie had so far taken no part in the conversation. Now, with a stretch of open road before him and the speedometer registering a hundred and twenty kilometres an hour, he glanced at Joey.

'What happened back there?' he said.

'Sorry, Adgie. I fronted Micky, George and Ronnie. They had a couple of minders there . . .'

'To cut a long story short,' said Francesca, 'the ungodly were smitten hip and thigh.'

'You mean we won,' said Adgie. 'Good enough.'

Now, after the heady events of the morning, the reaction began to set in. The soft suspension of the Citroen ironed out the uneven surface of the highway and the scuffling of the giant tyres had a hypnotic effect on its occupants. As Adgie exacted the best possible performance from his vehicle, driving smoothly and effortlessly, Joey leaned back in his seat and closed his eyes. His example was soon followed by the three in the rear seat.

Joey opened his eyes as Adgie was negotiating a potholed street on the outskirts of Murcia.

'How are we doing?' he said to Adgie.

'About another sixty miles to Alicante. Hour an' a half.'

Francesca lifted her head from Ace's shoulder.

'I could do with a cup of tea and a pee,' she said. 'What about it?'

'Sure,' said Joey. 'Pull in when you see a decent place, Adgie.'

A decent place presented itself as they entered the Spanish equivalent of a High Street in Murcia. It was largely plate glass, chromium and formica, constructed with the tourist in mind. Francesca entered first, followed by the rest of the team and, as they seated themselves at a table, an unmistakably English voice greeted them from the rear of the premises.

'Good afternoon madame, gentlemen.'

The owner of the voice emerged and proved to be a middle-aged Englishwoman in a flowered print dress equipped with a beaming smile.

'Hello,' said Francesca. 'I bet you can give us a nice cup of tea.'

'Indeed I can.' Her smile broadened as she went on. 'I can also give you some home-made scones with cream and jam. How does that sound?'

'Just the ticket,' said Francesca.

Their welcome set the scene for the pleasant half-hour which was to follow, during which it transpired that the English lady was the owner of the establishment, a widow who had sunk her savings into what all her friends predicted would be a dismal failure.

'As a matter of fact it's turned out very well,' she said. 'I've no complaints.'

Neither had her most recent customers. Even Adgie, who was hard to please in the matter of a good cuppa, pronounced himself well pleased. At the end of their short but pleasant stay Joey settled the modest bill, adding a handsome tip which he was at pains to explain was 'for the benefit of the staff', which saved embarrassment all round.

They came to Alicante in the early evening and booked in at the Grand on the esplanade which, Adgie assured them, was the best hotel on that part of the coast. He was proved to be right. The rooms, each with its private bathroom, were large, well-furnished and very comfortable. When they assembled in the lounge for a drink before dinner, Francesca was ecstatic.

'Wouldn't mind spending a week here,' she said.

Joey put the kybosh on that suggestion. 'The sooner we get out of Spain the better,' he said. 'We're not out of the wood yet. Keep your eyes skinned.'

They enjoyed an excellent dinner, although they were aware that they were the cynosure of all eyes. They were indeed a strangely assorted company, one black man, three white men and a beautiful girl who seemed to have no attachment to any of them. Quite a few eyebrows were raised among the British contingent and there must have been some low-voiced comments passed. Francesca took it all in her stride.

Joey had suggested an early night, but Francesca was in a lively mood.

'Isn't there a local night-spot, Adgie?' she said. 'You know. Guitars and flamenco and all that sort of stuff.'

'Well, yes,' said Adgie. 'Called the Castillo. On the top of the hill. Real gipsy stuff.'

'Come on, Joey,' said Francesca coaxingly. 'Let your hair down. Let's have a basinful.'

In the result they packed themselves into one of Alicante's large but ancient taxis which transported them to another world, an orgy of strumming guitars, stamping feet, hand-clapping and the sharp staccato of castanets. The Castillo

Santa Barbara was an old Moorish edifice perched on a hill on the outskirts of Alicante and the huge room in which the performances took place was sparsely furnished with rough wooden tables, but the action on the large stage was electrifying. Francesca was captivated. When the time came for them to return to the hotel she was reluctant to leave.

'We've got a long day ahead tomorrow, Duchess,' said Joey. 'I won't be happy until we've crossed the frontier.'

'Where do we go from there?' she asked.

'We'll see,' said Joey.

The following morning when they met for an early breakfast, Joey sprang his surprise.

'What about taking the car on to Paris?' he said. 'Spend a day or two there and then fly to London.'

Francesca was delighted with the idea. 'Lovely,' she said. 'I can do a bit of shopping.'

'Don't see why not,' said Ace. 'I haven't eaten real French grub for a long time.'

The Weasel needed no persuading and Adgie, as ever, was ready to obey orders. Joey put in a call to Malaga and, as a result, was informed that he was free to take the Citroen to Paris or anywhere else for that matter. Any charges would be billed to him in London.

The road from Alicante to the Franco-Spanish border hugs the coast for the greater part of its length. Joey took his seat beside Adgie and Francesca sat between Ace and the Weasel in the rear. Though they were all aware that they were not yet out of danger, their mood was relaxed. The minor bruising they had sustained in the fracas at the villa was only a memory.

They swept through Benidorm, a Southend-on-Sea set down on the Costa Blanca, Adgie expertly threading his way through a one-way traffic system that seemed to have been designed to baffle even the most experienced driver. As they emerged on the road to Valencia a glorious vista over the Mediterranean opened up, a vast blue expanse of ocean on which a few fishing boats bobbed lazily. A faint smudge on the horizon indicated the presence of Ibiza, one of the smaller of the Balearic Islands.

The Citroen ate up the miles as they negotiated Valencia, from where the road ran close to the shore as far as Tortosa, where the river Ebro empties itself into the sea. Joey, dozing in his seat, was roused by Francesca's plaintive voice from the rear.

'I'm hungry,' she wailed. 'What about some lunch?'

Adgie, who was also feeling the pangs of hunger, came in on cue.

'There's a place up 'ere on the right. Just before Tarragona,' he said. 'Not much to look at. The grub's good.'

Joey turned to him with a laugh.

'How come you know so much about this part of the world?' he said.

'Used to do one or two runs 'ere,' said Adgie.

Joey did not pursue the matter. There was more to this little man than met the eye, he thought. Adgie, for his part, said no more but put his foot down. Fifteen minutes later he brought the car to a halt before a small and unpretentious building overlooking the sea. A weatherbeaten sign proclaimed it to be El Paradiso. It appeared to be quite deserted save for a large man with a seafaring look about him, who was seated on a bench beside a large wooden table. As the Citroen disgorged its occupants, he looked up. His eyes lit up on seeing Adgie and he rose to his feet.

'Ola, señor,' he bellowed. 'Mucho time no see.'

Adgie waved a hand. 'Hi, Paco,' he said. 'Amigos. Comidas. OK.'

'O bloody K,' replied Paco. He gestured toward the table. 'You eat outside?'

'Let's do that,' said Francesca. She turned to Paco and shot a few questions at him in rapid Spanish. The big man was delighted.

'Momento, señorita,' he said, and disappeared in the direction of the kitchen, re-appearing a few minutes later with a large pail containing a variety of fish, some of them still wriggling. He addressed an enquiry to Francesca.

'Bueno,' she said, and turned to her companions. 'He says he'll cook us up a meal. Fresh fish, potatoes, salad. All right?'

There was a general nodding of heads, save for Adgie.

'Paco knows what I want,' he said.

They arranged themselves round the table as Paco once more did a disappearing act. Very shortly there emerged from the interior of the building a young man carrying a snowy tablecloth under his arm, which he proceeded to spread over the scrubbed boards. Paco brought out a half-dozen bottles of the local white wine, ice-cold from the refrigerator, and a bottle of San Miguel which he placed in front of Adgie.

The meal was ready in an incredibly short space of time. It took the form of an enormous wooden platter bearing what must have been the total contents of the bucket which Paco had shown them. Some of the fish were fried, others plainly boiled. Bowls of freshly-made mayonnaise, large containers of potatoes, boiled and fried, and a huge dish of salad made their appearance. Adgie received special treatment, a plate of fried fish and chips being laid in front of him.

'Blimey,' said Joey, 'there's enough here to feed an army.'

'We are an army,' said Francesca.

In the event, the food was so palatable that little was left. Joey and Francesca drank sparingly but Ace and the Weasel managed to get through four bottles of the local wine which Ace pronounced very drinkable. Adgie contented himself with the one bottle of beer. Large cups of strong black coffee completed the repast.

'If everybody has finished we'll get on the road,' said Joey. 'Ask him for the bill, Duchess.'

Francesca turned to Paco, who was hovering nearby.

'La cuenta, por favor,' she said.

'Mille pesetas, señorita.'

'A thousand pesetas,' said Francesca to Joey.

'Five quid! For that lot?' said an amazed Joey. He pulled

out his wedge, selected a five thousand peseta note and gave it to her.

'Tell him to keep the change,' he said.

'Don't do that,' said Adgie quickly. 'He's a Catalunian. He's asked a fair price. He don't want no more.'

Joey peeled off a green, which Paco accepted with a smile. Whether he had understood Adgie's interjection or not was a matter of conjecture. He appeared to be well pleased.

Back in the Citroen, Adgie refused Ace's offer to take the wheel.

'No offence meant,' he said, 'but I prefer me own driving.'

As the afternoon wore on, the miles rolled away. They made one stop at Gerona for a cup of tea. Crossing the border at La Junquera was, as Adgie had said, no problem. On the Spanish side the uniformed official didn't even rise from the canvas chair in which he was lolling, but waved the car through with a gesture that said 'don't bother me'. The French official was rather more formal.

'Quelque chose à déclarer, messieurs et 'dame?' he enquired.

'Rien,' said Francesca.

He saluted and waved them on with a 'bon voyage'.

They drove into Perpignan in the early evening.

The large room of the villa in Gibraltar was a meeting place well known to the eight men now gathered there, all having assembled at short notice. At the head of the table sat the man from Detroit and the others had taken their places in order of precedence. Reading clockwise, the well-dressed aristocratic figure on his left was a highly-placed member of the Metropolitan Police. Directly facing him sat two men, one a coarse-looking individual with small eyes deep-set in a florid face, the other a suave character with a habitual smile lingering at the corners of his mouth. The other four, patently junior members of the organisation, sat together as though finding strength in close association. The man from Detroit opened the proceedings.

'This meeting has been called in something of a hurry,' he began. 'For that I must apologise, but swift action is imperative. The head of our operation in Great Britain has been murdered and one of his best men on the distribution side has been delivered anonymously to the police with sufficient evidence to ensure that he will be sent to prison for a very long time. There is nothing we can do for either of them. According to our friend from Marbella,' he went on, inclining his head towards the man with the piggy eyes, 'the man responsible for these outrages is an ex-criminal, now in the private investigation field, by the name of Bello.'

One of the junior members spoke. 'We all know him,' he said, indicating with a sweep of his hand his three colleagues. Between them they controlled all crime in the London area. 'He's a hard case. Done a lot of bird. They call him England's Toughest Villain.'

The piggy-eyed man broke in. 'He was with us once. We got him over here so we could put him out of the picture. All we've got to show for it is one dead and four seriously injured.'

He shifted his position in the chair to ease the pain in his broken ribs. His neighbour, one of Britain's foremost lawyers, took up the story.

'I know this man,' he said. 'Do not underestimate him. He has brains, he is tough and resourceful and as cunning as a fox.'

The man from Detroit showed a trace of annoyance. 'What are you talking about? One man. Against our organisation which is in a position to bring down governments? Let's have no more of this nonsense. This man has declared war on us. He cannot be allowed to live.'

There was silence round the table. Each man considered the implications of the sentence of death passed on someone known to them as 'one of ours'. The piggy-eyed man broke the silence.

'That's it, then,' he said.

'It is agreed. This man Bello must die,' said the man from Detroit.

There was a chorus of assent. They all rose. The man from Detroit held up a restraining hand.

'Let there be no mistakes,' he said. 'Make the necessary arrangements. Bello must die.'

9. *The Mafia*

The team made a landfall at the Georges Cinq hotel in Paris in the early evening. Adgie had made good time after an early start from Perpignan, covering the four hundred odd miles in ten hours. He had chosen what he referred to as the scenic route over the Massif Central, a mountainous region of strange and wild beauty where every bend in the narrow winding roads opened up new vistas of heath and crags which seemed to stretch to infinity.

'Not a bad motor, this,' said Adgie to Joey as he whipped the Citroen through a tricky series of twists and turns on the descent to Clermont Ferrand.

'Good as the Jag?' said Joey. He received a grunt in reply.

Their rooms had been reserved by a phone call from Perpignan and, as was to be expected, they were luxurious in the extreme. After a bath and a change of clothing the five foregathered in the lounge to make plans for the evening.

'Had a word with a friend of mine. One of the top jollies over here,' said Joey. 'He's invited us to join him for a scout round the hotspots.'

Adgie had ideas of his own about the way he would spend the evening.

'Leave me out,' he said. 'I got other plans.'

'Like getting the bad water off your chest,' said the Weasel. 'Mind if I join you?'

'You're welcome,' replied Adgie.

In the event it was Francesca, Ace and Joey who went to the rendezvous with Joey's friend. As their taxi deposited them on the pavement outside La Rotonde in Montparnasse, a tall, elegant figure rose from his seat on the terrace and came up to them. He embraced Joey warmly.

'Joey, my old friend,' he said. 'How are you?'

His English was perfect, his accent that of an Oxford don.

in the course of business. He lived in luxury on the holiday isle of Jersey and controlled the operations of a number of off-shore companies whose purpose was to launder the vast amounts of skim money which flowed in a seemingly endless tide across the Atlantic. He was well-known as an influential and highly-placed member of the Mafia to those whose business it was to know such things. Joey decided to pay him a visit.

To decide was to act. Joey made a couple of telephone calls to a couple of friends in the Dale who were as tough as old boots and game for anything, as a result of which, on his arrival at Heathrow that afternoon, Joey was met by a half-dozen of London's hardest villains.

Before taking a taxi to the airport, Joey had put Francesca in the picture.

'Have to pop over to Jersey for a couple of days,' he said. 'Private business. Look after the shop while I'm away.'

'I'll do that,' she replied.

In one of the lounges at the airport, over a round of drinks, Joey briefed his little mob. His remarks were short and to the point.

'I've got a meet in Jersey. It's a bit iffy. If it comes on top, you'll have to perform. OK?'

There was a chorus of assent.

'Right. They're calling the flight now. Let's go.'

There was a minor hitch at Customs. The most formidable-looking member of the mob, a huge man whose face, criss-crossed with scars, had earned him the nickname of 'Tramlines', was selected for special treatment by one of the officers.

'Would you mind stepping this way, sir?' said the Customs man.

'What for?' said Tramlines truculently.

'If you please, sir,' said the official.

Scenting possible trouble, which was the last thing he wanted at this stage of the game, Joey bustled up.

'Anything wrong, officer?' he said.

'Nothing at all, sir. A routine check. If you'd wait in the departure lounge I'm sure your friend will join you shortly.'

Sure enough, Tramlines was back with them within minutes.

'No trouble?' queried Joey.

'Just give me a rub-down, that's all.'

There were no more delays. They took their seats in the aircraft and were on their way to their destination.

The world-wide communication system at the service of the Mafia is speedy and efficient. The older mafioso, given to fairy-tale description, called the international network the 'piccole voci' or Little Voices. The departure of one Joey Bello, accompanied by his gang of heavies, had been noted at Heathrow and the Little Voices had relayed the information to Jersey. That intelligence was in the hands of certain interested parties on the island before the landing wheels of the aircraft lost contact with the tarmac.

It may have been merely coincidence but, as the team were passing through the lounge at Jersey airport, two nondescript-looking men walked up to Tramlines.

'Excuse me, sir,' said the elder of the two. He flashed a warrant card. 'We're police officers. What's the purpose of your visit?'

''aving a break for a coupla days. All right?'

The younger officer took no part in the short conversation. He cast his eyes over the group as though committing their descriptions to memory.

The older man shot a keen glance at the deeply-scarred face. He had come across tough handfuls before.

'I see, sir. Very well. Have a pleasant stay.' He emphasised the word 'pleasant'.

Rooms had been reserved for the party at a small hotel very near St. Helier. On the short drive from the airport through lanes where the white painted houses were in startling contrast to the green and well-tended gardens with their riot of flowers, they skirted St. Aubins Bay, a splendid vista of blue sea and golden beaches beneath them.

The two taxis drew up before the hotel and the travellers disembarked. As they queued up to sign the register, Joey took a brief look into the lounge which was adjacent to the reception area. The young man who sat there idly turning the pages of a newspaper could have been an innocent holiday-maker but, as their eyes met for a brief instant, Joey knew what he was and why he was there.

In his room Joey made a telephone call. The voice at the other end of the line said 'Hello'.

'Hello, Arthur,' said Joey.

'Who's that?' said the voice.

'Joey Bello.'

'Hello, Joey,' said Arthur Parr. 'What are you doing in Jersey?'

Joey chuckled inwardly. You know what I'm doing in Jersey you sod, he thought. Aloud he said, 'Bit of business, Arthur. Thought I'd give you a call. Can we have a meet?'

'Of course, Joey. Why don't you come up to the house? Say tomorrow morning. About eleven.'

'I'll be there,' said Joey. He hung up.

In the small bar of the hotel the team gathered for a drink before dinner. A few words from Joey served to put them in the picture.

'Got a meet on tomorrow. It might be a bit dodgy,' he said. 'I don't reckon there'll be any trouble. Just the same, be ready for anything.'

He did not need to explain further. Joey had bought their loyalty for as long as he paid the bills, and he was the guv'nor. There was little conversation as they ploughed their way through an adequate meal in the dining room. Afterwards they made a short tour of some of the bars in St. Helier and retired comparatively early to their respective beds.

The residence of Arthur Parr, a man of considerable wealth and a respected member of Jersey's exclusive community, where money was the golden key that opened all doors, was a luxurious mansion overlooking the bay at St. Brelades. Arthur himself opened the door in response to Joey's ring on the doorbell.

'Come in, Joey,' he said. 'Nice to see you.'

He led the way into an enormous sitting room whose furnishings were in keeping with the general aura surrounding the house.

'Sit you down,' he said. 'What would you like to drink?'

Joey was not prepared to engage in the social niceties. He knew what he had come for and did not propose to waste time.

'No thanks,' he said. 'Too early for me.'

'Very well,' said his host. His urbane manner was not in the least shaken by Joey's refusal of hospitality. 'You wanted the meeting. What's on your mind?'

Joey went into the attack. 'Let's not mess about, Arthur,' he said. 'You know why I'm here. There's a contract out on me. Why?'

'You know why, Joey,' said Parr. 'I don't need to explain.'

'All right. I settled a personal matter in London. I got a call from Micky Brown and I went over to see that mob of thieves' ponces on the Costa del Sol. They had a pop at me and they came off worst. That's all there is to it.'

'No, Joey. That's not all there is to it. What you have done is to take out the head of a drug distribution network in London. Then you go over to Spain and have a ruck. You knock hell out of Micky Brown and his lot. One of them is dead. It can't be overlooked.'

Joey exploded. 'The hell it can't be overlooked. My name is Bello, but I'm not one of your comic-opera ice-cream merchants who shit themselves when somebody says omerta. I don't give a fuck who I'm up against so long as I know who they are. Who are they, Arthur?'

Parr regarded his questioner gravely. 'First of all, it's not my department. I handle finance, nothing to do with drugs. Look, there's a slim chance. I can fix a meeting with the top man in Detroit. After that it's up to you.'

'Can you call off the dogs until I've had this meet?'

'I can do that. You'll have to go over to the States. Leave it to me for the time being. I'll fix the meeting and give you a bell. I can't promise anything, but I'll do my best.'

There was no more to be gained by prolonging the conversation. It was significant that Parr did not ask for a number where he could get in touch.

'I'll wait to hear from you,' said Joey.

'Do that,' said Parr.

Back at the hotel Joey gathered his forces around him in the bar.

'We'll be going back to the smoke this afternoon,' he said. 'As for now, we'll go out and have a nice lunch. You can all relax. The heat's off.'

Over lunch, now that the tension had been removed, there was a general air of conviviality. A few jokes were told to the accompaniment of some raucous laughter and Joey, himself conscious of the temporary absence of the threat that had been hanging over his head, joined in the general celebrations. On the plane the holiday mood evaporated to some extent and, by the time the party reached Heathrow, it was back to business as usual. At the barrier he parted company with the gang after handing a roll of notes to their leader.

Adgie was on the spot to meet him.

'The car's just outside,' he said.

'Hang about,' said Joey. His attention had been attracted by the banner headlines on an evening paper on view at a news stand. He picked up a copy. 'HARLEY STREET DOCTOR ARRESTED' shrieked the large print. Beneath it appeared a report that police had visited premises in Harley Street that morning and arrested a prominent specialist who was taken to Marylebone police station. The report went on: 'Doctor Matthew Gill was charged with procuring female persons for immoral purposes. He was remanded on bail to appear before the magistrate tomorrow morning'. This, thought Joey, is a performance I'm not going to miss.

Turning the pages of the paper as the Jag sped towards London, Joey noticed a less prominent item of news tucked away on an inside page. It conveyed the information that a senior police officer in the Metropolitan Police had been suspended from duty pending enquiries into alleged irregularities.

'Well done, Duval,' said Joey half-aloud.

'What's that?' said Adgie.

'Just a thought,' said Joey.

Matthew Gill paced the floor of his consulting room. It was late in the evening. The bottle of Hennessy XO on his desk had been untouched an hour ago. Now it was almost empty.

His normally clear and logical mind, now muddled with drink, was unable to cope with the catastrophe which had overtaken him. He saw himself and his career in ruins, reduced to penury and divorced forever from his life of luxury. No more nubile girls to whip, no more consorting with his perverted friends in high positions, no more heady excitement as he discovered newer and more erotic paths down which he could wander. The prospect was completely unacceptable.

He stumbled across the floor to the shining trolley on which the instruments of his profession were neatly arrayed. With great deliberation he picked up a hypodermic syringe and slowly tested the action. From a cupboard on the wall he took a small bottle and pierced the plastic cover with the point of the needle. Holding the bottle upside down against the light he drew back the plunger of the syringe until it was fully charged.

He sat in the comfortable chair from which he had issued advice to his many fashionable patients. He had no advice for himself. He rolled back the sleeve of his coat and slowly squeezed the poison into his veins.

10. *New York*

The vapour trails behind Concorde as it flew above the weather from Heathrow to New York, lost themselves in a dim haze as the aircraft burst through the sound barrier. In the cushioned comfort of a first-class seat Joey stretched his legs out, leaned back and closed his eyes. In a matter of four hours or so he would be in the Big Apple and meeting face to face the man who had passed a death sentence on him.

He could have travelled on an ordinary scheduled flight but, conscious of the watchers who reported his every movement, he chose to travel in style. Although not given to morbid imaginings, he was now aware of the possibility that he might not use the return half of his air ticket, but that prospect lay in the future. The immediate present was of far greater concern.

His thoughts dwelt on the happenings of the past few days. He felt no compunction over the widely-publicised suicide of Matthew Gill, nor about his share in the events that had led up to it. What *was* a source of satisfaction to him was the telephone conversation he had had with Duval. The gist of it was that Finch had been nicked, remanded in custody despite an impassioned plea for bail, and was due, in Duval's opinion, to go down for at least five years. The DCS had thanked him for his co-operation. Joey's mischievous reply to that was to the effect that he had only done his duty as an honest and upright citizen.

Reflecting on the events that had led to his present position, he had no regrets. He had behaved according to his ideas of what was right and proper, exacting an eye for an eye and a tooth for a tooth and occasionally a life for a life. If the same rules by which he had lived were now to be operated against him, he would not complain. Yet he did not accept tamely and without question the proposition that sentence of death could be passed on him by an unknown person in a far-away place. He had wanted a confrontation, he had got it, and now all that remained was to face the enemy and see who came off best.

The sign above his seat requested him to fasten his seat-belt and the Concorde descended through the clouds to a smooth landing at John F. Kennedy airport. Carrying only hand luggage, he passed Customs inspection very quickly. At the Immigration desk he presented his passport to the gimlet-eyed official. The document was genuine, the photograph was undeniably that of the holder and the non-immigration visa, occupying almost a full page, had been obligingly supplied by the US Embassy. Cognisant of the fact that the United States of America, having a full complement of home-grown criminals, did not welcome imports from foreign shores, Joey had adopted another name.

The official flipped through the pages of the passport and gave Joey a searching look. What he saw obviously satisfied him. He went through the usual rigmarole – what is the purpose of your visit, how long do you propose to stay – then handed the passport back to its possessor.

'Thank you, Mr. Greville,' he said. 'Have a nice day.'

The taxi transporting Joey to the island of Manhattan slid smoothly into the flowing traffic of the three-lane highway. Ahead he saw the well-remembered towering skyscrapers, monuments to the American dream, symbols of man's desire to reach the clouds. He remembered the avenues and streets that carved the massive buildings into blocks, thronged with scurrying crowds reduced to the stature of ants by the enormous masses of steel and concrete surrounding them. There had been a time when the gutters of those streets ran with a mixture of blood and alcohol during the Prohibition era, as rival mobs fought to establish their supremacy, when the names of the leaders of gangs were household words. Joe 'The Boss' Masseria, undisputed ruler of Little Italy and head of the Unione Siciliane; Dutch Schultz, whose real name was

Arthur Flegenheimer, a convert to Catholicism from his original Jewish faith; Meyer Lansky and his partner Benjamin 'Bugsy' Siegel who gave birth to the infamous Murder Incorporated, which eliminated opposition on a strictly cash basis.

Their names were legion and have passed down in history. 'Lucky' Luciano, 'Uncle Frank' Costello, Louis 'Lepke' Buchalter, 'Don Vitone' Genovese, 'Scarface' Al Capone, their names read like the cast list of an Italian comic-opera. Yet there was nothing funny about any of them. To a man they were cold-blooded murderers who slaughtered their friends and their enemies with dreadful impartiality.

Those were the days of brutal executions in public. The streets, restaurants and even barber-shops served as killing-grounds. Innocent bystanders who got in the way of a hail of bullets died beside the criminals. A Thompson sub-machine gun was no respecter of persons.

Out of the evil seed sown in those far-off days grew the wild and dangerous flower now known internationally by one short word. Mafia. The influence of this organisation stretches to every corner of the globe. It taints and corrupts whatever it touches.

It was into this lion's den that Joey had elected to wander. The Big Apple, he thought. Well, it's big all right, but it's certainly got a nasty worm in the middle.

The taxi set him down at the Waldorf Astoria, where his accommodation had been reserved. The driver, a laconic New Yorker who had not uttered a single word during the journey, accepted his fare and a tip with a grunt. Inside the hotel Joey was dealt with smoothly and efficiently by a highly competent staff and whisked up to his one-bedroomed suite on the fifth floor in a matter of minutes.

He had just finished having a wash and brush-up when the call came. He picked up the handset.

'Mr. Greville.' It was a business-like voice, cool and impersonal.

'Yes,' said Joey.

'You have an appointment with Mr. Angelo Nero in exactly one hour's time. You will be picked up by car at your hotel in thirty minutes. Please be ready.'

The caller rang off. Blimey, thought Joey, that was impressive, though he was in no doubt that the exercise was intended to impress. What was of paramount importance to him, however, was that at last he had a name. Angelo Nero. What did it mean in English? From his scrappy knowledge of Italian he dredged up a rough translation. Black angel, he said to himself, and it wasn't a bad description either. Wasn't Satan an angel before he was despatched to the nether regions?

He had certainly heard the name before. During the gambling boom in the sixties, when casinos were springing up like mushrooms all over London, American expertise from Las Vegas and Atlantic City was an inevitable import. George Raft, the ageing Hollywood actor, fronted an operation at the Colony in Berkeley Square. Croupiers with American accents arrived in London in a constant stream, which went into reverse when the authorities discovered that these enterprising gentlemen had not troubled to apply for work permits. Junkets were organised on the other side of the Atlantic and hordes of gamblers poured in from all over the States, reinforcing the British Treasury with much-needed dollars.

Joey remembered that British mobsters were not slow to put a finger in this lucrative pie. Billy Hill, the Kray twins and the Richardson brothers climbed onto the bandwagon and enjoyed what could only be described as a wonderful ride.

During this time the name of Angelo Nero cropped up on many occasions. He did not enjoy the publicity accorded to such as Meyer Lansky, but he was beyond doubt a power behind the wily machinations of the Mafia as they infiltrated the British scene. It was apparent that, since that time, his influence in the upper councils had gone from strength to strength and he had become a leading figure in the international drugs traffic, a position which had accorded him wealth and privilege almost beyond belief.

This was the man with whom Joey was shortly to have a face-to-face confrontation.

The long black limousine with darkened windows stood at the front of the Waldorf Astoria. The concierge himself ushered Joey into the rear compartment and, as soon as he was seated, the car moved off. The partition between driver and passenger was firmly closed, but Joey was not particularly anxious to engage the driver in conversation. He was now committed to the venture he had undertaken. He needed no other company than his thoughts.

The driver appeared to be taking a roundabout route to his destination, but Joey judged they were proceeding downtown as they passed a few familiar landmarks. After some twenty minutes or so the limousine came to a halt before an office block in the Wall Street district. No sooner had it stopped than a man, who had been waiting on the sidewalk, stepped forward and opened the door.

'Mr. Greville.' It was a statement rather than a question. Joey nodded.

'Would you come this way, please?' He led the way through the doors, which worked automatically, and across a carpeted foyer to the lift. Two big, hard-looking men were standing by a desk. They gave Joey a searching look.

The high-speed elevator shot the two men rapidly to an upper floor. Joey deduced that it had been designed to serve that floor only, for there were no indications of access to intervening landings. His guide led the way from the lift to a door immediately opposite, on which he knocked softly and, in response to a call from within, he opened the door and ushered Joey into the presence of Angelo Nero.

It was a large office, sparsely but pleasantly furnished. The curtains were drawn and soft wall lights bathed the room in a rosy glow. The man sitting behind the large desk, which was bare but for a battery of telephones, did not rise nor did he extend a hand in greeting.

'Sit down, Mr Bello,' he said.

Joey sat in an easy chair, leaned back in a relaxed attitude and crossed one leg over the other. He surveyed the man opposite him, the strong, sun-tanned face with its mane of white hair brushed back from an intelligent forehead, the slightly prominent nose and the well-moulded mouth.

Nero started the proceedings.

'Before anything is said, I am aware that you have a reputation for violence,' he said. 'May I make it quite plain that you would be a dead man before you could lay a hand on me.'

'Point taken,' replied Joey. 'Anyway, I didn't come here for a battle.'

'Why did you come?'

'I wanted to see the man who had put out a contract on me, face to face, and ask him why.'

'Surely you know the answer to that, Mr. Bello. You killed the head of our distribution network in Britain, you were responsible for the imprisonment of one of his assistants, you went to the Costa del Sol and attacked a number of your ex-colleagues, causing serious injury and the death of one of them. There is only one answer. You must pay the penalty.'

'Are you interested in what I've got to say?'

'Certainly. You would not be here otherwise.'

'All right. The man Brandon. I had a personal matter to settle. I settled it. Too bad it had to be one of your men. So far as that gang of thieves' ponces on the Costa del Sol is concerned, I went on a meet with them. They told me they were going to put me away for good. There was a fight. They lost.'

A tiny smile lurked at the corner of Nero's mouth.

'You express yourself very well, Mr. Bello.'

'I tell it the way I see it.'

'What do you expect me to do about your situation?'

Joey's reply, about which he had thought deeply in anticipation of the question, came without hesitation.

'I don't give a monkey's. Everybody's got to die sometime. I'd like to put it off as long as possible, but . . .' He shrugged his shoulders.

'You showed considerable courage coming here.'

'Think so? I only did what had to be done. What had I to be afraid of? You're only human.'

'A good point. It's one that people in my position sometimes overlook. I must say I am surprised. I expected to meet some Cockney villain who would lick my boots and beg for his life.'

'Not my style, mister,' said Joey.

'I must say you impress me, Mr. Bello. I feel it would be a shame to end so promising a life. Tell me. If I were able to make your peace with the men on the Costa del Sol, would you consider taking over the job that Brandon – er – relinquished?'

'Like a shot,' said Joey. The first and second fingers of his right hand were firmly crossed.

'Very well. You will hear from me. The car will take you back to your hotel.'

The interview was over. The die, for what it was worth, was cast. For Joey only one thing mattered. He had fronted the man who had ordered his execution and walked away from it.

He came out into the main hall of Terminal 3 at Heathrow. Customs and Immigration had presented no problems. First class passengers on Concorde are not normally regarded as suspect by officialdom. He scanned the waiting crowd for the familiar face of Adgie to no avail. It was Francesca who came up to him as he passed through the barriers. Her face, devoid of make-up, was white and peaked.

'Where's Adgie?' he said. Instinct told him that something momentous had happened.

'Bad news, Joey,' she replied. 'Let's go and sit down somewhere.'

He stood stock-still. 'Don't bugger about, Duchess,' he said. 'Let's have it.'

'Adgie's been hurt. Badly. He's in intensive care. I can't tell you the whole story here. Come on.'

Without waiting for a reply she strode off towards the nearest lounge. Joey had to follow her. She chose a secluded corner and sank into a seat. Joey followed suit. Without preamble she plunged into a recital.

'It was early this morning. Harry was on duty. He heard a commotion outside. Turned on the closed circuit monitor. They got out of a van, four of them, masked up. They were carrying Adgie. Two men held him up against the front door. The other two nailed him to the door, long nails through his hands and kneecaps . . .'

She broke down. As tears came into her eyes, she clenched her hands tightly together in her lap. The knuckles showed white. Joey did not move a muscle.

'They crucified him,' he said tonelessly. The rage began as a fire in his guts and flowed through his entire body. He shook slightly and his head moved from side to side as if searching for someone or something on which to vent the anger that consumed him. Thoughts ran riot through his head, poor little bugger, he never did nobody any harm, why pick on him, the bastards, the bastards . . .

Abruptly he said to Francesca, 'Where's the car, Duchess?'

'I've brought the Jag. It's in the car park.'

'Let's go.'

'The hospital?'

'Where else,' he said.

Francesca drove speedily and efficiently down the motorway to London. No words were exchanged. She concentrated on driving, Joey was occupied with his thoughts. At the hospital they were shown almost immediately to the intensive care unit, where they were met by the staff nurse.

'Your friend's condition is stable,' she told them. 'He's undergone surgery but he hasn't come round yet. Would you like to have a word with the house surgeon?'

'Please,' said Joey.

The house surgeon was a perceptive Scot who had seen it all. The bizarre nature of his patient's injuries came as no surprise to him. He was cheerfully optimistic.

'Could be worse,' he said. 'Whoever it was did this gave him a severe beating before they hung him out to dry. Ruptured spleen, several broken bones, internal injuries, knife wounds to head and body. What did he do for a living, by the way?'

'He was my driver,' said Joey.

'It'll be a long time before he sits behind a wheel again. There'll be problems with his hands and legs. Question of articulation.'

'I want him to have the best,' said Joey. 'Could he be treated privately?'

'Wouldn't make any difference. He wouldn't get any better treatment. The National Health Service may be tottering but it's not on its last legs.'

They were interrupted by the staff nurse.

'Your friend has come round now,' she informed them. 'You can go in and see him. He won't be very bright. Don't stay too long.'

'Thanks,' said Joey. He turned to the doctor. 'Is there anything I can do?'

'Not a thing. Just leave it to us.'

The hospital bed was not particularly large but the tiny body of Adgie occupied only a small part of it. Just his head and his arms were on view. The swathe of bandages covered the whole of his face with the exception of his eyes and his mouth. Joey, no stranger to the aftermath of violence, felt a sudden surge of pity.

'Wotcher, Adgie,' he said.

From what he could see of the mouth Adgie had managed a smile.

'Don't worry, son. You'll be all right.'

One of the plastered arms made a slight movement of acknowledgement. The staff nurse, who had been hovering in the background, broke in.

'I'm sorry, sir, I think you should leave now. I suggest you come again tomorrow.'

'Thanks again,' said Joey. 'Come on, Duchess.'

They drove back to the house in Park Lane, where Joey questioned Harry on the events of the morning. He confirmed the story which had already been told by Francesca.

'Notice anything about any of them?' enquired Joey.

'They wore dark blue overalls. They were all masked up. I'm sorry. I didn't have a chance to do anything.'

'All right, Harry. There was nothing you could do. So what happened then?'

'Called the ambulance. They got Adgie down and rushed him off.'

'What about the Old Bill?'

'Oh, they came round. What could I tell 'em?'

'Nothing,' said Joey.

'That's right.'

Joey turned to Francesca. 'Let's call it a day, Duchess,' he said. 'See you tomorrow.'

'I don't have to tell you how I feel,' she said.

'No, you don't. I feel the same,' he replied.

London's Notting Dale has spawned a special breed of men. They are known as barrow boys, though they range in age from seventeen to seventy. As sharp as needles, streetwise and working on a simple principle that anything they sell must show a profit, they plied their trade from barrows in the Portobello street market, dealing in any commodity for which there was a public demand. That some of the goods they sold had conveniently 'fallen off the back of a lorry' caused them no embarrassment. They claimed them, they sold them and added the proceeds to the considerable wedges which they all carried.

Some of the older ones, steeped in tradition, wore a typical off-duty uniform, a plain blue suit with an obligatory white silk scarf knotted at the neck, the ends tucked into their braces. A favourite resort for a select band was a small public house within a stone's throw of the Portobello Road. They were known throughout the Dale as the Wild Bunch, they consumed enormous quantities of light ale and they spoke a language which was incomprehensible to the outsider.

Joey came to the pub around eight o'clock in the evening. He felt a need to be among his own kind, people whom he understood and who understood him. Most of all he wanted to blot out the picture of the small, pain-racked figure lying in a hospital bed to whom he was unable to give either help or comfort.

The first person he saw was his elder brother Nobby, who greeted him as though they had last seen each other only yesterday. The rest of the Wild Bunch were also very much in evidence. To the accompaniment of a slightly out-of-tune piano, Danny Mac was beating out a rhythm on a table top with a brace of empty light ale bottles. Nat the Nylon King, little Artie and Bernie the Bolt, their heads close together, were deep in discussion. Big Bob crooned the words of the song being played in a rumbling bass. Also present were the two Jacks, Roger the antique dealer and Ronnie the florist. They greeted Joey with a wave or a smile.

The first large Scotch went down very well, as did a second and then a third and Joey began to relax, though the memory persisted. He stood at the bar with Nobby by his side as they indulged in desultory chat about family matters. Though Nobby must have known about the tragic happening in which Adgie had been involved, a natural delicacy prevented him from mentioning it.

The evening wore on as Joey pursued his objective, which was quite simply to get completely and absolutely legless. His mental state was an inevitable result of the strain under which he had laboured during his visit to New York, coupled with the shock that awaited him on his return. Try as he might, he could not shake off the mental picture of the times he had sat beside Adgie as, the tiny hands resting lightly on the wheel and the agile feet beating a tattoo on brake, clutch and accelerator, the little wheelman had whisked him out of many a tight corner.

The legal hour which spelled the cessation of drinking for

the majority of the patrons came and went. Closing time meant nothing to the Wild Bunch. They enjoyed the privilege of 'arfters', a concession granted by the landlord to favourite and free-spending clients. The doors were locked and drinking continued. Nobby looked at his brother with some concern. He had never seen him in this state before.

'Coming round my place, Joey?' he asked.

Joey regarded him owlishly as he hung on to the bar for support.

'Gotta get home,' he mumbled and hiccuped loudly. 'Things to do. C'mon. Taxi.'

He stumbled to the door, Nobby's supporting hand under his elbow. Outside in the fresh air he staggered and almost fell.

'Want me to come along?' said Nobby.

Joey shook his head with an effort. Now he wanted to be alone, to crash out and sink into merciful oblivion. Nobby hailed a cruising cab.

'G'night, Nob,' he said. 'See you later.'

The cab decanted him at the house in Park Lane within minutes. He stood on the pavement for a few seconds groping in his pocket for the gadget which would open the door. In the normal course of events he would have taken a look up and down the street, but in his present state caution was the last thing on his mind.

Harry was waiting in the hall.

'All right, Joey?' he asked.

'Yeah. Yeah. Going to bed. G'night.'

He staggered up the stairs and into the sitting room of his private quarters. Collapsing on to the settee, he fell back and closed his eyes. A curtain came down over his mind, blotting out all recollections of the past few days. He slept.

He had no idea of the time when he was awakened by Harry shaking him by the shoulder. He sat up abruptly. Sleep had cleared the fog of alcohol from his brain. It was dark outside but a sudden brilliance illuminated the room as a tongue of flame licked the windows. There was an acrid smell of smoke in his nostrils.

'Fire,' yelled Harry. 'C'mon. Gotta get out.'

They rushed to the landing, where they were met by billows of smoke rolling up from below. They wasted no time on words. Harry hoisted Joey on to his shoulders. Joey shot back the bolts of the trapdoor leading to the roof, clambered out and reached down a hand to assist Harry. Together they crouched on the rough asphalt.

'What happened?' said Joey.

'Two mobs. One at the front, one at the back. Smashed the windows, chucked Molotov cocktails in.'

Joey ran to the parapet and looked down on to Park Lane. Through a swirling haze he saw three dim figures sprinting towards a car parked a short distance from what had once been his front door. He drew back as a huge gout of flame erupted from the ground floor and soared towards him.

'Harry,' he shouted. 'This way.'

As they scrambled across the rooftops to safety, they heard the wail of sirens in the distance. They circumnavigated three more roofs before they came across a fire escape which led to ground level. They finally emerged in a side street. Joey laid a hand on Harry's arm.

'Hang about,' he said. 'You never know.'

They allowed a decent interval of time to elapse before rounding the corner into Park Lane. They crossed to the opposite side of the road and joined a group of spectators who were watching the London Fire Brigade at work.

'Looks like a goner,' said Harry.

Joey nodded. The fire had taken a firm hold and roaring flames mounted towards the dark sky. Hundreds of gallons of water poured onto the conflagration. As the two men watched, the roof on which they had been standing only a short while before suddenly collapsed, and the walls crumbled in on themselves. What had been a solid Georgian house was being rapidly reduced to a pile of rubble.

'No point hanging around,' said Joey. 'Get hold of the boys and girls. You know the Bolinbroke?'

'Yes,' said Harry.

'Get them all round there at eleven.' He looked at his watch. 'I'm going to finish my kip.'

Joey was up and about at ten o'clock. The night porter at the Bolinbroke had recognised Joey at once, despite his smoke-blackened face, and showed him to a vacant room.

'Won't disturb Mr. O'Malley now. I'll tell him you're here in the morning,' he had said.

He had telephoned Francesca and Ace, and was assured that they would be with him at eleven. All he had to do now was wait. He sipped at a cup of well-sweetened black coffee and began to give some thought to the prospect before him. The fire, coming as it had on top of everything else, was a real facer which had deprived him of everything except the clothes he was wearing. The cunning of his enemies was only too apparent. If he didn't die in the fire, they figured, he would be demoralised and an easy target for the final coup. Well, that's where they're fucking well wrong, he said to himself.

The staff of the now defunct J. Bello Investigations arrived in a body. As they seated themselves on the chairs which had been brought up by the obliging porter, Ace and Francesca made their appearance. Sitting on the bed, Joey opened the proceedings.

'You all know what's happened,' he began. He addressed his remarks to his six employees. 'The business is finished. I'm sorry. That's the way it is. If any of you need a few bob to tide you over till you get something else, give me a shout.'

Harry spoke for all of them.

'We've been well looked after,' he said. 'We've had a word. If there's anything we can do to help, you've only to say. We're all prepared to work for nothing till you get back on your feet again.'

'Thanks, but it's too late for that,' said Joey. 'The

The police and the ambulance crew arrived together.

'My God,' said one of the ambulance men as he surveyed the scene of carnage. 'This is a job for a hearse.'

One of the bodies stirred slightly and a low moan issued from the battered face. There was a look of astonishment on the face of the ambulance man who had not so far spoken.

'Get him in the wagon, Jim,' he said. 'This bugger's still alive . . .'

